# Voices of Freedom

## CONTEMPORARY WRITING
## FROM UKRAINE

EDITED BY:
KATERYNA KAZIMIROVA &
DARYNA ANASTASIEVA

 8TH & ATLAS PUBLISHING

⊛ 8TH & ATLAS PUBLISHING

8th & Atlas Publishing
911 Walnut Street
Winston-Salem, NC 27101

www.8thandatlaspublishing.com

*Voices of Freedom: Contemporary Writing From Ukraine* was
inspired by interviews published by www.craftmagazine.net

This book was ethically and responsibly manufactured by
Lightning Source.

Cover design by Vitalina Lopukhina

print ISBN: 978-1-7377181-6-1
ebook ISBN: 978-1-7377181-7-8

To all the people of Ukraine
and those who value freedom the most.
This book will not stop the war, but it
will explain what we are fighting for.

# CONTENTS

# A NOTE FROM THE EDITOR

Recent events have brought Ukraine to the attention of the world. Much of the global citizenry has been gripped by Ukraine's struggle and courage. This is a fight for the most fundamental and important value, one that resonates especially with those living in a democratic society—freedom.

*Voices of Freedom: Contemporary Writing from Ukraine* is a collection of Ukrainian writing that aims to introduce the English-speaking world to 27 of the most iconic as well as emerging living writers whose work is shaping contemporary Ukraine. These are leading intellectuals and moral authorities for the Ukrainian people, whose voices and opinions have helped to synchronize the internal compasses of Ukrainian society in the struggle for the freedom of their country. Through poetry, short stories, and essays, this collection demonstrates that the desire for freedom and the struggle to achieve it is a theme that cuts across generations of Ukrainian writers, and is a central preoccupation of Ukrainian society.

The volume opens with a poem by one of the last leading

lights of the "dissident movement" of the Sixties, *Ihor Kalynets*. The volume continues through the works from the 80s, 90s, and 00s, when the modern Ukrainian literary canon began its formation. It reaches its zenith in this generation's canonical figures who have just recently begun to receive wider acclaim (including such luminaries as *Oksana Zabuzhko*, *Yuri Andrukhovych*, and *Serhiy Zhadan*), who have developed the themes of a young country's struggle to rethink and overcome its Soviet past, including topics of internal freedom and right of self-identification. And finally, there is the younger generation of writers from the last two decades with their cutting-edge, vital, original, and energetic prose and poetry, which both chronicles and contends with the multifaceted impact of the Russian war.

This collection demonstrates the unique style and artistry of contemporary Ukrainian literature. The curated poetry is an instant reaction to the events taking place today, which speaks directly to this current moment and the national psyche. Poems of war are gut-wrenching, but they often help us find purpose in a fragmented, unstable world and even inspire us to rebuild what we have lost. The short stories sensitize readers to Ukraine's indivisible history and the present. These are accounts about the memory of generations, choices and transitions, self-irony, friendship, love, and the powerful significance of home. These stories and novellas, whether written in the traditional mode of realism, in the style of global modernism, or in the style of magical realism, all represent a single continuous story showing the paths, lives, and values of the Ukrainian people who have amazed the world with their courage. The essays showcase the voices of contemporary Ukrainian intellectuals, providing analysis and reflection on what is happening in the present, showing historical connections and parallels, and shedding light on the origins and triggers of the war on the mental level.

This volume will appeal to a variety of audiences. Book-buying patrons who have been touched by images and narratives of Ukrainian perseverance and resilience in the face of Russia's brutal war will find here an open window into the lives and minds of the real people represented in these depictions in human terms. Literary-minded individuals, who may indeed have a zealous attraction to European literature, will find here an introduction to a distinct and rich written tradition, a vibrant and increasingly essential corner of the European literary canon. Internationally minded folks who follow world affairs and foreign policy will find on these pages a deeper understanding of the divergent perspectives and priorities of the people behind events featured in the news. A rising generation of cultural creators and innovators will find within this anthology kindred spirits and deep connections with dazzlingly imaginative counterparts living and working on the fringes. And finally, all readers of this work will encounter, in spite of daily despair, hope for the future, and a conviction that our way of life is worth pursuing and preserving at all costs.

The Eastern European country of Ukraine has a long history, a proud identity, a rich culture, and indeed a bright future. Its past and current sagas are marred by tragedy. However, its literature is devoted to overcoming historical trauma and postcolonial identity. As this collection shows, the Ukrainian spirit is also filled with humor and humanity, patience and perseverance, inspiring readers to believe in the eventual triumph of life over death and truth over lies no matter what—lessons from which societies facing populist and authoritarian threats may also learn. Ukraine was already on the cusp of breaking out as the next "big thing" on the world map of pioneering contemporary culture—much like other parts of Eastern Europe in the 1990s and early 2000s. Now the world is finally interested, Ukraine is seen and heard, but it is also fundamental for it to be understood. It is time for Ukraine to tell its story—not through the state-prescribed Russian rhetoric that has shaped its colonial image for centuries, but through the words of Ukraine's cutting-edge, contemporary literary and cultural leaders, who Ukrainians themselves turn to in order to give voice to their struggle for freedom. The collection that follows is the story of Ukraine, in the voice of Ukrainians.

– Kateryna Kazimirova
Managing Editor
*April 2022*

# Voices of Freedom

## CONTEMPORARY WRITING
## FROM UKRAINE

EDITED BY:
KATERYNA KAZIMIROVA &
DARYNA ANASTASIEVA

# IHOR
# KALYNETS

A poet, novelist, former political prisoner, and dissident (b.1939, Khodoriv; Lviv oblast today), Kalynets is a laureate of international and national prizes and an honorary member of the PEN Ukraine. In 2015 he was nominated for the Nobel Prize in Literature. He is an author of 17 poetry collections, divided into cycles in the two-volume *The Awakened Muse* (Warsaw, 1991) and *Slave Muse* (Baltimore-Toronto, 1991). Kalynets wrote the first nine collections before his imprisonment in 1972; the next eight were penned during imprisonment and exile. Before the restoration of Ukraine's independence, his collections were published only by self-publishers from the Ukrainian diaspora in the USA and Europe.

One of the most gifted Ukrainian lyricists of the 20th century, Kalynets is a representative of the poets of the generation of "the Sixties." His work revived the baroque language of writing, appeared through neo-baroque and Ukrainian folk art, and had a pronounced influence on the formation of modern Ukrainian poetry. He is a prominent representative of Ukrainian modernism. In his texts, deep poetic thinking, sophisticated language, and gentle eroticism appear alongside social protest, archaic power, and cultural resistance to Russian expansion.

Together with his wife, poet, and dissident Olena Stasiv-Kalynets, he was repressed in the early 1970s and received six years of detention in harsh camps and three years of being exiled. He served his sentence in Perm concentration camps alongside well-known Ukrainian dissidents. After returning from the Soviet forced labor colonies, Kalynets no longer writes poetry. He instead works on translations of fiction, in particular between Ukrainian and Polish, republishes selected poems, and writes popular fairy tales for children.

Kalynets has retained his spirit of resistance, as he protested against the unlawful decisions of the authorities during the Yanukovych era and more recently has been actively involved in cultural resistance to Russian aggression since 2014.

The recipient of an honorary doctorate from the Ivan Franko National University of Lviv, Ihor Kalynets lives and works in Lviv.

## 18.

having gained wind
from white sailcloth
like fish from nets

having taken
a shard
of unresolved yearning
out of the eye of a stranger

having robbed my beloved
of her sleepless sleep

having plucked
another day
of illusion
from the steppe of the soul

having ignored
haughtily
the baroque arsenal
of journalism

having clung with my ear
to the wall of the day
as if to the wall of a prison cell

having stolen
faded flowers
from the dictionary's herbarium
having beheaded
a thistle
in a metaphor meadow
and having filed
the fern flower phrase
to the shape
of a full moon
having signed a self-inflicted
free verse
verdict

I become convinced
thrice a day:
if you are not
a poet's
denunciation

what are you then
poetry
?

*1971*, from the book *Vers Libre Sentence*

*Translated from Ukrainian by Svetlana Lavochkina*

Svetlana Lavochkina is a Ukrainian-born novelist, poet, and translator. She has lived in Germany since 1999. Her work has been published worldwide. Her novella, *Dam Duchess*, was chosen as runner-up in the Paris Literary Prize. Her novel, *Zap*, was shortlisted for Tibor Jones Pageturner Prize, London. Both books in German translation were published by Voland & Quist to national critical acclaim. Lavochkina's verse novel, *Carbon*, was published in 2020 by Lost Horse Press, USA. In 2022, *Carbon* in Ukrainian self-translation was announced a prize-winner in Lviv's International Literary Competition, "Winged Lion." Since the onset of the war in February 2022, Lavochkina has been continuously raising awareness of Ukraine in germanophone mass media.

# YURI
# IZDRYK

Novelist, poet, essayist, translator, artist, and musician (b.1962, Kalush), Izdryk is the author of several full-length novels, including *Wozzek* (1997), translated into English in 2006, *Double Leon* (2000), and *AM™* (2004). Moreover, he is the author of several poetry collections, including one translated into English in 2019 and published by Lost Horse Press collection *Smokes*. His creative work also consists of a number of essays, novellas, and short stories as well as articles related to literary and cultural studies. Izdryk is an author of the conceptual magazine project *Chetver* (*Thursday*), which, since 1989, played a role in launching the careers of many contemporary Ukrainian authors.

Izdryk is a versatile artist and one of the creators of the Stanislav phenomenon, a group of postmodernist post-Soviet writers, and one of the most influential representatives of Ukrainian postmodernism. He is a prominent figure in the avant-garde scene and alternative literature. He also works in easel painting, graphics, and collage and is an active performer. Izdryk signs his books only with his last name and is considered one of the most original and mysterious Ukrainian authors. His prose and poetry can be full of melancholy, lyricism, and waltz melody; and at the same time, his works have an influence on *batyarism*—the phenomenon of Lviv urban culture at the beginning of the 20th century, represented by cunning, ill-fated lovers of freedom, with their own peculiar moral code that often conflicts with written laws.

In 2014, after the beginning of Russian aggression in Crimea, he temporarily stopped writing poems. At his concerts and events, he supports home-grown resistance to the Russian war against Ukraine.

He lives in Kalush, Ukraine.

## WAR

Two travelers arrived.

One of them called himself a preacher. "So, preach," I said to him. He replied, "Ship your grain across the sea; after many days you may receive a return. Invest in seven ventures, make it eight; you never know what disaster may come upon the land. If clouds are full of water, they pour rain on the earth…"[1] I had to set the dogs on him— real preachers are silent, after all.

The second asked for a drink.

I gave him water, and he sipped a little and set off muttering either thanks or curses under his breath. Out of curiosity, I followed after him, but he noticed me, turned and said with innocent holiness, "Blessed are you when people insult you, persecute you and falsely say all kinds of evil against you because of me. Rejoice and be glad, because great is your reward in heaven, for in the same way they persecuted the prophets who were before you."[2] Disappointed and ashamed, I returned home. Later on, dirigibles began to fly across the sky setting off lights and fireworks. And the postman brought letters from the front.

---

1 Ecclesiastes, 11:1-3 [New International Version].
2 Matthew, 5:11-12 [New International Version].

And so, The Final War took place. And it was a place for it. I too received a summons, and, having packed the essentials, resigned myself to fight.

War begins with the military latrine. The first display of patriotism is that you defecate with everyone together in a common pit. Buried excrement scattered throughout the land becomes a source of fertility for future generations—as do the burials of human bodies later on.

The second manifestation of patriotism consists of endless transport. Trains shuttle you day and night. There's the search for boiled water at unfamiliar stations, the suffocation of lying on the top bunk in the sleeper car, and the rhythm, the rhythm that gets into your blood like a pulse. The absence of this rhythm during stops is unbearable and can lead to madness. Constant changes to the route bring on déjà vu.

The third manifestation of patriotism is the constant anticipation of battles. The time of inactivity in the trenches and tents belongs to the most difficult trials on the front line. Inaction breeds desire, desire leads to hope, hope spawns confidence that the war will end and pass you by. And, somehow, just when everyone begins stitching on their demobilization armbands, the fighting begins. They go happily into battle, straightening their wooden bodies along the way. Combat brings a sense of relief, and in some cases, release. And death.

It's true that weakness caused by constant waiting and anticipation gives rise to an Asthenic Syndrome.[3]

Medicine does not have an answer to this ailment.

---

3 Hypochondria, or black melancholia.

And Asthenic Syndrome will surely cut down two or three post-war generations.

But it was in the military hospital that I met Anna.

We crossed paths in the hospital corridor with large painted windows on one side and a row of doors on the other. I walked, trying not to step on the black tiles—an engrained mental defect, a rudiment of childhood. Anna was approaching, as always with her face lowered—a habit developed in overly-male surroundings. At that point, I didn't know her name. In her hands she carried something concealed under a white cloth. The distance between us was closing. I forgot about the black squares—the way you sometimes forget about pain. It's just that I hadn't seen a woman in a long time. We passed each other in the corridor with large painted windows on one side and a row of doors on the other.

Probably, it was the force of my desire that knocked the load out of her hands, and I turned to the glassy ring of metal to see various medical paraphernalia falling in a rattle. I watched as shiny, sharp, and dangerous instruments of medical torture flew across the white and black squares: ampules burst, spraying drugs and poisons; rubber bulbs jumped like frogs away from their destinies as butt plugs for soldiers; tourniquets squirmed like snakes; the ruthless points of needles bent sharply; tweezers danced on thin legs falling into a frenzy; clamps convulsed and scalpels sliced rolls of cotton bandage; mirrors cracked; spirals and springs shuddered in convulsions; the creaking artificial joints of prosthetics teetered for balance; saws and drills shrieked; bones and teeth crumbled; anatomical remains poured out from unfurling bandages and purple adhesive wrap. In what was not, I saw what was. We both stooped to collect the mess, growing a little closer, moving toward one another from opposite sides of the chessboard. *e2 to e4*: the best move to start the game. *e2 to e4*: how will she respond? Anna cried, without raising her head, and the tears, her tears, which had no pathway to flow down her face—where there are channels provided by nature or God—gathered at the tip of her nose and dripped one after the other to the floor, mixing sometimes with medicine and then with poison, slipping away in different streams with floating silver drops. Was it mercury from different thermometers? It definitely was. *e2 to e4*. I still did not know then that she was Anna. I was clearing some kind of birdseed from under the radiator, and Anna, my Anna, was collecting the sharp glass of broken syringes, *e2 to e4*. We approached each other steadily, performing this one and only most successful and well-calibrated move, *e2 to e4*. *e2 to e4* we crawled along the black and white squares of the hospital corridor until just before her tears fell on my hand and our knees—though I was most afraid of offending her with my approach—until just before our knees touched, and I finally saw her face and chapped lips, which, barely moving, said "thank you." I kissed her wet eyes and only those wet eyes, taking no more notice of chapped lips or the drops gathered at the tip of her nose. I saw the things that I could not, because in our hands we held instruments of torture—we feared the slightest movement with them. Anna, I said, Anna.

And the corridor filled with people.

*1995*

YURI IZDRYK

*Translated from Ukrainian by Grace Mahoney*

Grace Mahoney is a scholar and translator of Ukrainian and Russian literature. She is a PhD candidate in the Department of Slavic Languages and Literatures at the University of Michigan and serves as the series editor of the Lost Horse Press Contemporary Ukrainian Poetry Series. From 2014–2015, she participated in the U.S. Fulbright Scholar Program in Ukraine as a Student Researcher. Her book of translations of Iryna Starovoyt's poetry, *A Field of Foundlings*, was published by Lost Horse Press in 2017. Her translations have also been featured in *AGNI*, *Alchemy*, *Apofenie*, *harlequin creature*, *Ukrainian Literature: A Journal of Translations*, and *Ploughshares*.

# YURI
# ANDRUKHOVYCH

An award-winning poet, novelist, essayist, and translator
(b. 1960 in Stanislav, modern Ivano-Frankivsk),
Andrukhovych is considered the patriarch of contemporary
Ukrainian literature.

Andruhovych is the author of six full-length poetry
collections, among them *Exotic Birds and Plants* (1991), *Songs
for a Dead Rooster* (2004), and *Letters to Ukraine* (2013); seven
novels including *Recreations* (1992), *The Moskoviad* (1993),
*Perversion* (1996), *Twelve Circles* (2003), *The Secret* (2007), *Lovers
of Justice* (2017), and *Radio Night* (2021); a collection of short
stories titled *Lexicon of Intimate Cities* (2011); and numerous
essays. His works have been translated into several
European languages. The novels *Recreations*, *The Moscoviad*,
*Perverzion*, *Twelve Circles*, the poetry collection *Songs for a
Dead Rooster*, and the collection of selected essays *My Final
Territory* are available in English translation. Andruhovych
is the author of Ukrainian translations of Shakespeare's
*Hamlet* (2008), *Romeo and Juliet* (2016), and *King Lear* (2021),
as well as an anthology of American "beatnik" poetry of
the 1950s–1960s, *The Day Mrs. Day Died* (2006).

In his youth, he founded the poetic group "Bu-Ba-Bu" (Burlesque-Bluster-Buffoonery), which played a fundamental role in contemporary Ukrainian literature. After the fall of the Iron Curtain in the 1990s, he became a co-founder of the Stanislav phenomenon, a group of postmodernist post-Soviet writers. As a postmodernist, he easily mixes genres; he combines reality with phantasmagoria, satire with lyricism, and eroticism with the irrational. He constantly experiments with language and symbols, employing irony and skillful hoaxes. His protagonists are bohemians in search of lost identities, who, as if in a kaleidoscope, discover the multidimensionality of losses and love.

Since the 1980s, Andruhovych has been involved in the national movement against the Soviet system, and since the independence of Ukraine in 1991, he has actively defended democratic European values. He was a participant in three Ukrainian revolutions: The Revolution on Granite, The Orange Revolution, and The Revolution of Dignity. After the full-scale Russian invasion of Ukraine, he actively participated in volunteering movements and spoke out against Russian propaganda.

He lives in Ivano-Frankivsk, Ukraine.

## UNDERGROUND ZOO

*Under the city live, as in fairy tales,*
*Whales, dolphins and newts...*

– Bohdan Ihor Antonych

Living under the city, whales. And newts.
And also, dolphins. In the twilight of the depths,
in the hollows where the black moon sinks,
where stone's been quarried from cavities,
they live, lampreys and moray eels,
sirens, octopi. And submissive
blind inflorescence of sponges and jellyfish—
in the shafts of the mines, in the pits of our souls.

Living under the city, lions, yellow and sleepy.
The hot grass hides them.
Flying zebras, antelopes, and horses
bloom on the bottom of pastures and savannas.
Living under the city, crocodiles too.
Entangled in the sweet veins of lianas,
shiver the shadows of monkeys or parrots.
And hundreds of hundreds of flies, ants, and toads.

Living under the city, wisents and aurochs,
their trumpets roar into the night like frozen copper.

Saigas and roe deers, stepchildren of nature,
graze on the edge of the night lands.
And mammoths, as obedient as cows,
and mastodons. Stone oakwoods
quiver because of them, tremble like warm mud,
they fled here from hunters.

Living under the city, people. Pilgrims
and burghers. Their wings in their sleeves.
The penny-prized, vicious circle of faded
amusements spins around again—
everything remains the same. Beer fests,
wedding fiddles, lanterns, horseshoes,
kisses, crying, love and darkness…

Under the city. Which is long gone.

*1989*

## SET CHANGE

Within the church they opened a train station:
waiting room, altar lamps, icons, and booths.
The crowded choirs buzz like a cauldron,
and female cashiers with mouths like fake rubies.
Restrooms and frescoes. The Christmas star
turned to ash like Mary dressed in black.
You open the altar gates like doors —
exit and walk down the first platform.

And there, trains and wind before rain. The light
from candles guttering like voices at a banquet.
We cluster around the car. And blowing a whistle,
a proletarian prophet in a red service cap.
Within the school they opened a hotel:
someone gets ready to sleep with somebody.
Wet stalactites pulsate from the ceiling,
high school girls crave cotton candy
and, twisting the channels of intertwined arms,
master the essence of the natural sciences.

Within the castle they opened a hospital:
there chivalry rambles in shabby pajamas
as if beaten by fire or plucked from a stake,
and they prepare a diagnosis like planning a murder.
Because at night in each of the dimly lit towers
chivalry's treated for shame. With hammer and nails.

Within the circus they opened a factory:
there a proud people fly over the lathes
in gaudy clown makeup from ear to ear.

Within the sky they opened a prison.
Within the body they opened darkness.
Within the spirit they opened bedlam.

*1989*

## BALLAD OF RETURN

When the traveler came back home,
passed the gates, crossed the threshold,
hefting on his shoulders the road and fatigue,
all the joys of this world landed at his feet.

He wasn't forgotten, they'd waited for him:
dinner with wine at a generous table.
Somehow, he didn't talk about distant berths,
locking unknown sadness between his lips.

And everyone wondered, and his wife
sighed in vain pursuit of sleep until morning.
But he kept watching there, behind the curtain,
where a star swam through the sky above the window.

*1982*

*Translated from Ukrainian by John Hennessy and Ostap Kin*

John Hennessy is the author of two collections, *Coney Island Pilgrims* and *Bridge and Tunnel*, and his poems have appeared in various journals and anthologies. He is the co-translator with Ostap Kin of *A New Orthography*, selected poems by Serhiy Zhadan; the work was a finalist for PEN America's Translation Award for Poetry 2021 and co-winner of the Derek Walcott Prize for Poetry in 2021. Hennessy also co-translated the anthology *Babyn Yar: Ukrainian Poets Respond* (forthcoming from Harvard Library of Ukrainian Literature/HUP). He is the poetry editor of *The Common* and teaches at the University of Massachusetts, Amherst.

Ostap Kin is the editor, and co-translator with John Hennessy, of *Babyn Yar: Ukrainian Poets Respond* (forthcoming from Harvard Ukrainian Research Institute), the editor of *New York Elegies: Ukrainian Poems on the City*, and the co-translator, with John Hennessy, of Serhiy Zhadan's *A New Orthography*, which was a finalist for the PEN Award for Poetry in Translation and co-winner of the Derek Walcott Prize for Poetry. He co-translated, with Vitaly Chernetsky, Yuri Andrukhovych's *Songs for a Dead Rooster*, a collection of selected poems.

# OKSANA
# ZABUZHKO

A major writer and intellectual of Ukraine, Zabuzhko is an award-winning novelist, poet, and essayist (b. 1960, Lutsk). She is the author of ground-breaking feminist works *Fieldwork in Ukrainian Sex* (1996, published in English translation in 2011) and *Museum of Abandoned Secrets* (2010, published in English translation in 2012). Zabuzhko, a professional philosopher and cultural researcher, most often works in the genre of non-fiction, and is best known for *Notre Dame d'Ukraine: Ukrainian women in the conflict of mythologies* (2007). Her work *And Again I Get Into the Tank* (2016) is a personal narrative about the war. In 2020, Zabuzhko presented to the English-speaking world her collection of short stories *Your Ad Could Go Here*. Her novels, short stories, essays, memoirs, and non-fiction are constantly republished and have been translated into more than twenty languages. Plays based on her works are performed on the stages of Western Europe and the United States.

The main themes of Zabuzhko's literary work are national identity, feminism, and the manifestation of gender roles. She is a master of long and thoughtful sentences and combines deep realism and melancholy with thorough historical research. Zabuzhko is provocative and revolutionary in her texts, elaborates on the post-colonial heritage and national traumas of Ukrainians, and at the same time offers a clear and accessible explanation of Ukrainian culture to the Western reader. As a guest writer, she has taught Ukrainian culture at world-renowned universities, including Harvard, Yale, and Columbia since the 1990s.

Zabuzhko's life and cultural and literary activities are characterized by fierce resistance to centuries-old Russian aggression. She participated in three Ukrainian revolutions: The Revolution on Granite (1990), The Orange Revolution (2004), and The Revolution of Dignity (or Euromaidan, 2014). On March 8, 2022, she became the first non-EU citizen writer to speak before the European Parliament, receiving a standing ovation.

## DEPORTATION

"This is no longer your home," the men with machine guns tell you. "Pack up, the transport is ready."

This message can come—has come, countless times—in different versions. For example, *You have two hours to pack* (or half an hour, or twenty-four hours—a difference, in this case, nothing short of existential). Or, *You are allowed two kilos of belongings per person*, (or five, or as much as you can carry), and every clarifying detail here is worth its weight in living flesh, each smells of breast-milk, of freshly baked bread, of baby hair and old photographs, of the conjugal bed, medicine, dried herbs in a sachet, the candle-wax splattered gods of the hearth—of that entire inalienable life of yours, fed into your blood by several generations, and out of which you now must snatch, with great precision, a few essential elements so that it can stay intact—and it's already fallen apart! You can throw together a new, portable, backpackable home for yourself, a snail's shell that would keep you whole. This is why it is in fact a very important question, the question of all questions perhaps, one the answer to which will say much more about you than hundreds of questionnaires and quizzes of the which-five-books-you-would-take-to-a-desert-island variety: *How much time would you need to pack if you found men with machine guns on your doorstep and they told you, get out, the transport is waiting?*

This is not a journey—a journey is something from which you return. It's not emigration—emigration is something you choose. At least you retain agency in your actions. Here, the key word is "transport," because you become cargo, a statistical unit of logistics on a mass scale, like a head of cattle, or a cord of wood. Someone else's invisible will has determined that you are to be uprooted, like a tree, from your one and only *home*, from the landscape of your tribal, genetic memory, as organic and tangible as a limb, to be transported across the map into oblivion and abandoned in an alien place. Now, they tell you, your home is here—put down new roots. If you can't, if you wither— well, that's your own fault.

Should the experiment be repeated on several generations, those subjected to it learn not to put down deep roots anywhere, ever. They learn to avoid becoming one with any place, like those unfortunate souls who had their first love brutally thwarted and spend their entire lives afraid of loving again. The instinctive, bone-marrow-deep memory of the original trauma of being uprooted blocks every subsequent attempts at rootedness, flashes a red alarm: a home of one's own (and, by extension, the protective concentric rings of one's village, city, and country around it) *is the thing that it hurts to lose*, so—no, please, don't make me, I'll have a light, portable home instead. This way, should the doors fly open and the strangers with machine guns step inside, you could pack, grab the essentials (your baby in the sling, your laptop in your backpack, your credit cards in your chest-pocket, you'll buy what you need wherever you're going, hurry, hurry, *the transport is waiting!*), and roll on with the wind, through cold, desolate space, not rupturing anything, no bleeding heart, no slashed flesh, having taught yourself to love not a point on the map but the distance between points, not the stasis, but the transition, not a place, but the motion: the road—the railway station—the airport. You're up for it—being a nomad, living out of a suitcase, for years, decades if you have to, blind to your environment, as a tourist is blind to the peeling, flee-stained wall-paper in hotel rooms.

One learns to recognize them—places that are unloved, land that had been robbed of true owners, villages littered with strangers' graves, places under the pall of anemia as if someone had pumped all of their blood out and injected them instead with someone else's, of incompatible type. The new, rejected blood cells are people, and their loitering in these places, among incomprehensible walls and neglected homesteads where other families' ghosts howl in the chimneys leaves an outside observer with a disorienting impression that all these people are, mentally, not here but elsewhere, someplace where, they secretly believe, their real life, their *own* ancestral Golden Age is being kept, with no expiration date or long-term penalties, on ice, awaiting defrosting. This faith of theirs stays with them as the smell preserved somehow at the bottom of their own grandmother's hastily (*You have two hours!*) packed suitcase. Even if nothing else could be preserved, taken along, this smell is forever—there is no home without it. Not even a portable home.

We catch whiffs of it in every corner of the world, at every latitude. The children, grandchildren, and great-grandchildren of the deported, we have spread over the surface of the planet like a new ocean, carrying with us our virus of acquired home-deficiency. We want to feel at home everywhere—and so we have homogenized, ironed out the universe into a few universally recognizable—and therefore (trans)portable—elements: the highway, the gas station, the McDonald's, the airport. We rely on disposable cutlery and cycle through domiciles and localities as we do through laptops and mass-produced winter coats. We have adapted quite well, when you think about it, nothing to complain about. The only thorn in our collective side is this smell.

It can overcome you without warning—it ambushes you in a snippet of an old tune, an accidental combination of colors, the sounds of a forgotten language. It's in the steam rising from a pot of food—oh yes, we are convinced this is *exactly* what it smelled like in the kitchen of our great-great-grand-home, recipes are always replicated from memory, aren't they, so the same food tastes the same no matter where it's cooked. Doesn't it? (The correct answer is, no, it doesn't, but it's better not to know this.) Movies, books, retro-styled cafes, historic reconstructions—we have spawned an entire industry of nostalgia, just so we wouldn't feel homeless. But the smell still visits us in our dreams, and can explode with sudden, awesome force, reverberating through the entire length, it feels, of that long-ago un-rooted trunk—and that's how you find a grown woman, a refugee from the occupied Donetsk, wailing and screaming at the stunned hospital personnel to dare not—*dare not!*—designate her a "migrant" in her new records, because she's no migrant, oh no, *she had driven her own car here.*

And you cry with her, you wail right along, disapproving looks from the check-in ladies be damned, because you know this: two or three generations ago, this woman's ancestors were brought to the Donbas to work the mines, like most of the locals to-be, precisely as official Soviet "migrants"—in a cattle car filled with other exiled *kulaks*[4]. They were lucky—my kin were taken out to much more distant lands, to Siberia and the Kazakh steppes, and the mines they dug there and the cities that grew, like polyps, around those mines are now falling into ruin without any help from the Russian army, by virtue of those lands restoring themselves to wilderness in the wake of the violence inflicted upon them by men—and there isn't anyone there who might look after the graves of those of my family's members who never came back.

The woman in Kyiv—the third-generation deportee—had come back. By herself. She drove her own car. And it doesn't matter that she was forced to do so—to pick up and go, albeit in the opposite direction this time—by men with machine guns (probably of the same brand as all those years before). The important thing is that she is no longer a piece of cargo, she has "her own car"—a perfect snail's shell, her portable home that she had managed to put together from the land that was never really domesticated, and thus never loved, and thus the land so bitterly, hopelessly, and frighteningly left *defenseless*.

---

4 Kulak means "a prosperous peasant." These were farmers who had larger farms, but mostly this term was used to label anyone who had more income than was considered "normal." Bolsheviks proclaimed them "class enemies." In the 1930s, the Dekulakization started—the policy of dissolving the kulaks as a class by sending them to Gulag, by deportation to distant provinces, or by physical elimination.

I can picture her driving. Through the rolled-down window, she could smell the smoke of burnt-out fires, the steam of field canteens at check-points, exhaust, and the breath of the spring steppe coming to life—the smell of home.

*2015*

*Translated from Ukrainian by Nina Murray*

Nina Murray is a Ukrainian-American poet and translator. Her translation of Lesia Ukrainka's *Cassandra* won the 2021 Ukrainian Institute London Prize for Ukrainian Literature in Translation. She is the author of five collections of poetry.

# IVAN
# MALKOVYCH

A poet, editor, and publisher (b.1961, Ivano-Frankivsk region), Malkovych is a laureate of national and European awards, in particular the highest cultural award in Ukraine—the Shevchenko National Prize in the field of literature (2017). He is the author of seven collections of poetry for adults, including *With an Angel on My Shoulder* (1997), *All Is Near* (2010), and *The Plantain* (2016), and has authored, edited, translated, and compiled more than thirty children's books. Malkovych's poems have been translated into many languages and presented in literary journals and online magazines. His poetry is metaphysical and homely, light and fairytale-esque, filled with Ukrainian symbols and intonations of a husband and father.

The founder, director, and editor-in-chief of the first private Ukrainian children's publishing house, A-ba-ba-ha-la-ma-ga (1992), Malkovych created the most popular book brand in Ukraine, which successfully competes on the international market. Malkovych's publishing house published in Ukrainian the bestselling seven-volume *Harry*

*Potter* series by J.K. Rowling. A-ba-ba-ha-la-ma-ga now also specializes in eclectic adult literature and recently presented the Ukrainian translation of Quentin Tarantino's first novel *Once Upon a Time in Hollywood*.

The publishing house has donated generously to the Ukrainian army, and Malkovych himself donated his Shevchenko National Prize money to families whose parents died in the war in eastern Ukraine.

He lives and works in Kyiv, Ukraine.

# IVAN MALKOVYCH

\*\*\*

I love recognizing you
on maps the world over
following your flight
on swiftly spinning
globes

my dear homeland
my touching comedy

you're not a bird or a little animal
or a cub
or a duckling
or a goose –

you're a beargoose

(here's another
ugly little duckling for you
up there in the sky hans christian)

with your head in europe
and your tail facing a nesting doll

(and your rear would be much plumper with voronezh
and kuban[5])

you run away
from that all-consuming nesting doll

---

5  References to Kuban and Voronezh, Ukrainian ethnographic
territories now part of Russia.

that smothers everyone with its kremlin
you run
but can't quite get away

hordes of nesting doll backers
running on foreign batteries
are lurking inside you

but here I am
squinting
and clearly seeing
you racing across the water
inhaling air –

your protruding wing
ready to take flight
you pick up speed –
fly –
sing –

croak –
and inspire us –

and awaken us
with your heart
you love us
with your wing

…but I'm worried about your left paw

*November 1, 2008; February 18, 2009*

# IVAN MALKOVYCH

\*\*\*

I want unconditional triumph, once and for all,
wild fortune and a welcoming world,
carols fluttering over us like flags,
and a sliding down a mirror-smooth path
        into a Christmas myth

For everyone to feel, once and for all, that God
is now with us and for us, and our wandering is over,
so we anxious ones don't fall asleep alone,
two backs turned toward each other,
        like two question marks…

…I gently kiss long-lasting fear from her,
        like from a fresco,
I tell her – don't be afraid, it's safe here
        because there's a Mesozoic plateau here.
My arms are robust, my chest shields you from the wind.
My tears are behind my eyes where nobody can see them.

*2015*

## LEONTOVYCH[6]

At Christmas time New York leisurely floats by
through the windows of a beige, mother-of-pearl Cadillac
festive snowy streets illuminated by shiny
people of various shades

he gets out of the car across from the Apple Store
        on 5th Avenue
and walks leisurely toward Rockefeller Center:
over there – across the street
        from the main Christmas tree –
there's a Christmas video installation on a giant wall and
        "Carol of the Bells" playing on repeat

Someone in the merry crowd recognizes him:
"Look, look, it's Mr. Leontovych, who wrote 'Carol of the
Bells'!"
"'Ukrainian Bell Carol,'" Leontovych said, smiling.
"Oh, yes, yes! Can I have your autograph?"
"A little selfie please!"
"…with us too!"
"Oh my God, it's Mr. Leontovych, the king
        of Christmas spirit!"
"Ya tak lyupyty vasha myuzik!"
Well, some of that was Ukrainian…

---

6 Ukrainian composer, author of the main Christmas song "Carol
of the Bells." The song was first introduced to the North American
audience 100 years ago on the 5th of October 1922 at Carnegie Hall.
Leontovych died tragically; he was killed in his father's house by a
Cheka agent who asked to spend the night in their house.

a slim man with a gray beard squeezes his way through
and they embrace fitfully
Leontovych turns toward the happy people
swarming around or taking pictures with him:

"Meet Peter Wilhousky, who wrote the English lyrics to
        'Carol of the Bells'...we're both from Ukraine..."
...
There I stand, among a pack of tourists, with tears
        streaming down my face...Freezing in mid-air
they bounce high off the cement sidewalk
and crunch under the feet of passersby

Leontovych recognizes me, steps toward me
extends his warm hands:
"what happened? why are you crying my friend?"
"oh don't ask maestro, I had a terrible awful dream..."
"well tell me and forget it – it's Christmas after all!"
"the dream was about...you, Mr. Leontovych..."
"me? then you must tell me!"
 "...I dreamt...that many years ago...in 1921...a secret-
police officer asked to spend the night at your house...and
before sunrise...no...no...I can't..."
"please go on, I'm not afraid of dreams..."
"...and before sunrise he...shot you..."

I'm shaking like I have a fever

Leontovych suddenly fades away
a blue chasm appears where he was standing

…

I close my eyes and open them again…

A swallow swirls down 5th Avenue…a merry
Mr. Leontovych is taking pictures again
with chattering fans…

It's as though I've emerged from a bloody tunnel:
"I'm so glad that was just a dream!" I whisper to myself.
"Just a scary, oh-so scary dream."

*January 5–6, 2016*

\*\*\*

I have too little hate
even my explosive enraged hammer
has rusted
I make do with mere disdain

I don't judge people by their downfall alone –
            because anyone can
slip into scum someday
I want to know how high someone sprang
whether they tried to get eight feet off the ground
and how pure their harmonics were

Because people populate in geometrical progression
yet the world empties and hollows out –
people prattlebabble and therianthropize –
humanity passed the peaks of its prosperity

There are so many of us that the essence of God
may have to be spread evenly among everyone
and that's why there's less and less essence
            in each of them

They're saying that in the night sky outside of Kyiv
a string of UFOs is moving south
(and I, an old skepticus, almost believe it)
forty round dots
lined up straight, with German severity
who are these concerned observers –
is it some sort of rescue mission?
I know:

God is preparing us for travels far away
He's the one who slipped us gadgets so we could
take our favorite books photographs paintings music
with us to unseen worlds –

but what should we do with our violins
and cellos – will there be
even more imitation there?

But You know
that despite it all
I feel good here
in Your earthly orchestra

so forgive me if I've ever asked You too adamantly
to shine on my stand
when I stop seeing
my sheet music

*May 5, 2020*

## SWAY THE SKIES

Like a pebble
flying and flying
off a mountain
into a deep, deep
bottomless lake
and – plop! – just like that your heart drops
when a child suddenly falls ill

And you're confused at first
and helpless
eager to act – implore the world
and sway the skies

Before sunrise
in the morning mist
I look out, hand on my forehead
men standing all over the world –
on mountains
on hills
even on balconies
and on trees
and on skyscrapers
all anxious and overwhelmed with love
tugging on celestial strings visible to them alone
straining to sway the skies

And all of a sudden
for a split second
the skies swoop down slightly

like a gigantic parachute
and then like the petals of morning peonies
white and pink
morning angels
sleepily slide
and slip slowly

still silly and disheveled
still sleeping mid-air like children
perpetually suspended
like during a pause by Amadeus

They touch down
and instantly
scatter among the ones they've chosen

You can never guess
whether they've all landed today
or whether somebody slept in and stayed in the skies
(because a weary child is crying here)

And then
vividly I see
it tangled in tall grass –
a gene running over
gasping for breath
the last one

*2020–January 2021*

IVAN MALKOVYCH

*Translated from Ukrainian by Reilly Costigan-Humes and Isaac Stackhouse Wheeler*

Reilly Costigan-Humes and Isaac Stackhouse Wheeler work in both Ukrainian and Russian and are best known for their renderings of novels by great contemporary Ukrainian author Serhiy Zhadan, including *Voroshilovgrad*, published by Deep Vellum, and *Mesopotamia*, published by Yale University Press. Wheeler is also a poet whose work has appeared in journals including *The Big Windows Review*, *The Peacock Journal*, and *Post(blank)*.

# VOLODYMYR
# RAFEYENKO

Ukrainian novelist and poet Rafeyenko (b. Donetsk,1969) lived and worked as a professor of Russian philology in Donetsk and wrote predominately in Russian until 2014. The author of eight books of prose and three poetry collections, he has won several prestigious literary prizes awarded to Russian-speaking writers. After the outbreak of the Russian–Ukrainian war, he was forced to move to Kyiv and start his literary career virtually anew. The first Ukrainian-language novel *Mondegrin*: *Songs about Death and Love*, about language and the experience of being a refugee in his own country, was translated into English by Mark Andrychyk and published by Harvard University Press in 2022. His novel about the war, *The Length of Days* (2017), translated from Russian to English by Sibelan Forrester, is forthcoming in 2022.

Rafeyenko is one of the most intellectually original Ukrainian writers. His prose is surreal, mystical, and absurd, drawing inspiration from the best examples of European romantic and modernist traditions (Gogol,

Kafka, Marquez). His novels take place between sleep and reality, his characters are fluid and unstable, and the plot moves with the rhythm of the language.

He lives and works in Kyiv, Ukraine.

## HARVEST

In the village, the apricot blossom is almost over, and the path leading to the old house is strewn with petals. The grass has grown tall and thick. There's a scent of damp earth, bitter white petals, tulips. The neighbors opposite are clearing their garden, burning branches. Smoke fills the shady, windy, lofty spaces between the trees; every five minutes there is a brief downpour of cold, fat raindrops. Then you can cup your hands, catch a little water and splash it on your face.

Strictly speaking, the garden belongs to somebody else. I enter quietly and sit under the canopy of the semi-dilapidated side entrance to the house. My forbears built this house, but very soon, in no time at all really, strangers will come and live here. They will live as if I was never here. As if it was not I who used to run along these paths with my ridiculous, long butterfly net, not I who woke in the night, feeling sad and lonely, and cried into my pillow, not I who absolutely worshiped Mama and Papa. They'll come here as if I never ever had a Mama and a Papa. As if my long, enchanted childhood, the beginning of my life, had never happened. They will roam all over this place, they will break up the old furniture, get rid of my old bicycles and toys, send my stamps, books, badges into exile on the "Mounds," they will scratch their heads when they examine my boxes of slides, which are the most fascinating thing in the world. "Puss in Boots," "Pinocchio," "Little Red Riding Hood." The new owner of the house will turn over the old slide projector in his hands and tut-tut. "Huh! I had one just like this when I was a kid." And he will throw it on the heap along with all the other crap that must be gotten rid of as soon as possible.

Well, so what? After all, he has to make a life here for himself. He didn't buy the house so that he could run about with a butterfly net. That would be quite a sight. He will cut down the plum tree, the pear tree and our two precious cherry trees, "because they're old." He'll completely demolish all the buildings, he'll raze everything to the ground. Naturally, he will slightly encroach onto municipal territory when he builds a new, six-foot high boundary wall of red brick. He will clean out the old well and have the most delicious water in the world. His very own water. But first of all, the very first thing he'll do is dig up all these warm garden paths, destroy the anthill, cut down the elderberry bush and the guelder rose, eradicate the peonies and the tulips. He needs the space to dig the pit for the foundations.

So, is there any point in waiting? Perhaps I could just surreptitiously pour some special substance over everything, so that it all turns to dust, burns up, disintegrates, gets blown away on the wind, disappears forever. I shouldn't, of course. Because, supposing I now burn it all to cinders, the purchaser won't pay the full price for scorched earth, for smoldering timber. He may not be too pleased if everything here has gone up in flames. Maybe he bought all this so that he could incinerate it all himself. And he'll be annoyed if someone else has beaten him to it.

It's more than likely. I mean, nowadays, it's very difficult to make categorical statements about people. These days, people have all sorts of ideas.

A better plan is to time things to coincide with his arrival. He'll drive here with his brand new bride, fresh from the altar, to show her the plot of land where their brand new house will stand. They probably won't come until the autumn, because all the paperwork and such still has to be done. He will drive up, and everything will be on fire, enveloped in flames. The roof has just started to blaze and is merrily showering sparks into the sky, the cherry tree is burning with a tang of cherry pain, bark and memories. The pear tree smells sweet, its branches are being burnt alive, juice seeps from them and sizzles, there's a north-westerly wind, it's autumn. The first droplets of rain patter onto his windscreen. And they seem to make the fire burn more brightly, more invitingly. Plump, juicy rain clouds float across the sky, the autumnal village opens itself up to the world, like an ancient living flower. The heat is so intense that the jars of pickles and preserves in the pantry fridge start to boil. Grandma Marfa Alexandrovna distractedly screws up her eyes at the icons and the clock, and whispers something. She threads her needle with a lovely thick strand from a ball of wool. She has heaps and heaps of these balls.

They are all of different colors, thick and warm. She makes wonderful rugs out of them. There's something stretched on the carpet frame, which, in a year's time, will have become a hand-made rug. As usual, I am sitting under this frame, which takes up the whole room, and playing in my own imaginary little house. Nowadays, perhaps, I don't fully understand the hidden meaning of this game, but I did, back then. I have a few sweeties in my hand, but I've already eaten a great many, so I'm feeling a little drowsy. Grandma always sings quietly to herself while she is working. Her songs almost always sound sad. These Slavic songs have something slightly unhinged about them, which listeners of all ages find irresistible. Irresistible and spellbinding.

Mama calls us to the table. Someone extricates me from under the carpet frame and carries me into the living room. And here we all are at the table. Mama, Papa, two grandmas, two grandpas. Papa and my grandfathers are just downing their first shot of vodka at the exact moment when the window catches fire, the glass panes shatter. The wind swirls into the house, smoke billows. My father starts telling a funny story and everyone laughs. Someone has slipped me a piece of cheese and I am nibbling at it sleepily. My brother is asleep in his pram. Flames dance on the table, casting a magnificent glow on the crystal shot glasses.

"Oh, what a beautiful sight!" says the new owner's wife. "Mm, lovely," says the owner, rather distractedly. He gets out of the car. He lights up a cigarette. "But what's going on there, in the living room?" he says, staring into the smoky flames. "Look, there seem to be people in there." "Don't be silly," she says cheerily.

"What do you mean, 'people'?" "Real, live people," he says.

A second window shatters, and a whistling draught blows the smoke out of the room, and fans the flames. Old framed embroideries burn on the walls, photographs, small paper icons, *rushnyks*.[7] The Saint Nicholas icon is the only one that doesn't burn. The metal icon cover, the riza, gleams more and more brightly. Fat drops of holy oil trickle down the saint's face and onto the ancient sideboard, picked up as a bargain in the long-vanished year of 1952.

"It's really getting quite chilly in the evenings," says Mama. "What do you expect, it's October," say the men folk, and pour themselves another shot. "October. It's always chilly in October." "They're forecasting snow for next week," says Grandma Lyubov. "Eat up, Vovochka, eat up," she smiles at me. "Oh come on now, Lyubov Zakharovna, what do you mean, snow?" objects my father. "This year the autumn will be long and warm. It won't snow for ages yet. But when it does, there'll be a hell of a lot of it." "Snow?" I ask. "Yes, my boy, snow." "And Grandfather Frost," I say. "That's right," says my father. "Grandfather Frost in person. The frostiest of all."

"Lyuda, there really *are* people in there," says the new owner. He kicks open the gate and tries to get closer, but fortunately it is already impossible.

The house is burning. And as in every real house, the only things that burn are the things that were non-essential, incidental. All those slide projectors and butterfly nets, certificates, letters, testimonials, absurd savings books and pension books, all that disappointment and pity, all those springs and winters, illnesses and misunderstandings, tears and regrets, all that accumulated pain and those endless recollections that nobody wants.

---

7 An embroidered or woven towel made of linen or cotton, part of Ukrainian traditional ceremonial cloth. Each region of Ukraine has its own distinctive pattern and style of embroidery.

Suddenly my uncle appears and goes past the new owner, straight into the burning doorway. "Don't get too close to the fire, Silly," he warns the new owner as he passes him. "You've still got two little girls to bring up." He looks at him for a moment and smiles. Pulling aside the burning door curtain, he disappears into the fire. "Yes, Misha," echoes the owner's young wife, rather distantly, "move further back. He's quite right about that. But what did he say about children?" "Be quiet, you silly woman," says the new owner. He is transfixed by what he can see through the window: my family is celebrating the coming harvest. There's my uncle, downing a shot of vodka as a forfeit for being late; there's my five-year-old self, standing up on Lyubov Zakharovna's lap; I'm looking through the window and giving a little wave. I am not just waving at him, I am taking leave of the world. "Goodbye, new owner," I say to him. "Goodbye forever."

*2009*

*Translated from Russian by Sara Jolly*

Sara Jolly is a literary translator based in London. Her translations include Igor Golomstock's memoirs, *A Ransomed Dissident: A Life in Art under the Soviets* (I.B. Tauris/ Bloomsbury, 2018), Alexander Etkind's *Nature's Evil: A Cultural History of Natural Resources* (Polity, 2021), and short stories in *Teffi's Other Worlds, Pilgrims, Peasants, Spirits, Saints* (Pushkin Press and NYRB Classics, 2021), edited by Robert Chandler.

# IVAN
# ANDRUSIAK

Ukrainian poet, author of children's books, novelist, literary critic, and translator (b.1968, Ivano-Frankivsk region), Andrusiak co-founded a group in the 1990s called New Degeneration, which had a considerable influence on Ukrainian literature. Andrusyak is acclaimed as one of the leading poets of the 1990s generation. He designed his own discernible poetic manner based on the use of metaphors and dense symbolism. Among the features of Andrusiak's poetic work, critics note fragmentation, collage, surreal displacement of planes, hermetic imagery, and introverted writing. Despite all this, the essence of a Ukrainian living in the real world, sometimes fleeing to the past and always dreaming of a happy future, is hidden under layers of coded vocabulary.

Since 2005, Ivan Andrusiak has turned to children's literature, where he experiments with genres and forms. Thematically, his children's books are about how to be yourself, to be aware of who you are and what you are; how to gain success and fulfill one's potential based on personal identity, not following someone else's. Since 2014, Andrusiak has been the main editor of the Fontan

Kazok publishing house (Fountain of Fairy Tales), which specializes in books for children.

Andrusiak's work has received several prizes and has been translated into twelve languages. In 2013, his book *Eight Days from the Life of Burunduk* was listed in the renowned *White Raven* catalog of the best children's books worldwide.

He lives in Kyiv, Ukraine.

## THE THIRD WORLD SILENCE

(excerpts)

\*\*\*

henceforth snow will no longer be white
henceforth it won't even be snow
only a dream in which quivering silence
stays afloat on the water

henceforth water will no longer flow
but will simply flee from wasteland to wasteland
and no one knows whom to flee
perhaps from water

the terrain is awash in a silence
thick to the eye
bitter to fingers
cold in the veins

it seeps into pores
forces cracks open
bites into shores

given the slightest of chances
it's already inside you

o
how resounding
this silence!

\*\*\*

once they buried the dead under thresholds
and all who
wished to enter
had to doff their hats
and bow

and silence stayed outside

God was the earth then
the earth heaven
and life upon it
abounded with stars
resembling roses

anyone wishing to come in
would light a star
and be seen from afar

and all knew that light was light
and silence darkness

now they release the dead with smoke
and God flees skyward
farther and farther

and the dead keep reaching out to Him
so that from here
it already appears
as if even God is beyond them

— a corpse

# THE THIRD WORLD SILENCE

\*\*\*

it was the first world
silence

so oppressive
that in the end God couldn't stand it —
He added clay
and kneaded the earth

but silence struggled through the earth
grew stronger
bubbled up
and burst

thus sound was born

and from that sound
came beasts
and birds
and beasts
and more beasts
and people

and they were happy with the silence
cavorted
clapped their hands
shouting so loudly
that the earth winced

and God listened to them
listened
and couldn't get enough

64

IVAN ANDRUSIAK

\*\*\*

when the doves flew south
a wall of white sun rose
across the sky
and wouldn't let them through

and the doves were at a loss
and went soft

and knew not where to fly
into the night or from it

and they folded their wings
and plummeted
into the naked sky

\*\*\*

and stone and amen there were
and amen smote with stone

*June 6, 2021–March 28, 2022*

*Translated from Ukrainian by Boris Dralyuk and Roman Koropeckyj*

Boris Dralyuk is a literary translator, poet, and the Editor-in-Chief of the *Los Angeles Review of Books*. He holds a PhD in Slavic Languages and Literatures from UCLA. His work has appeared in the *Times Literary Supplement*, *The New York Review of Books*, *The New Yorker*, *London Review of Books*, *The Guardian*, *Granta*, and other journals. He is the translator of Isaac Babel, Andrey Kurkov, Maxim Osipov, Mikhail Zoshchenko, and others, the editor of *1917: Stories and Poems from the Russian Revolution* (2016), and the author of *My Hollywood and Other Poems* (2022).

Roman Koropeckyj is a professor at the Department of Slavic, East European, and Eurasian Languages & Cultures at UCLA, where he has been teaching since 1992. He received his BA in Comparative Literature from Columbia University in 1976 and his PhD in Slavic Languages & Literatures from Harvard University in 1990. Koropeckyj is the author of *The Poetics of Revitalization: Adam Mickiewicz between Forefathers' Eve, part 3, and Pan Tadeusz* (East European Mongraphs, 2001) and *Adam Mickiewicz: The Life of a Romantic* (Cornell University Press, 2008) as well as articles on Polish, Ukrainian, and Russian literature.

# TARAS
# PROKHASKO

Prokhasko is one of the leading prose writers in post-Soviet Ukraine, whose books have received prestigious Ukrainian and international literary prizes (b. 1968 Ivano-Frankivsk). He studied biology at Lviv University, specializing in botany. This influenced his writing as well: in his works, he often tries to recreate the inner affinity of the human soul with the plant world. A person of versatile talents, Prokhasko also worked as a columnist, a radio operator, a video operator, an editor, a bartender, a radio host, a forester, a teacher, a screenwriter, and a gardener.

Prokhasko's prose is characterized by a meditative tone and concentration on details. Many of his works contain biographical elements and are extremely rooted in the locality, but this does not simplify his prose; on the contrary, it makes it very frank and brings it closer to an intimate confession. Prokhasko is mostly known for working in the style of magical realism. His main work, the novel *NeprOsti* (*The UnSimple*, 2002), is a kind of "alternative history" of the Carpathians in the first half of the 20th century.

Prokhasko's prose has been translated into a number of languages. The following publications feature his works in English: the novella *Necropolis* (in *Two Lands New Visions: Stories from Canada and Ukraine*, 1998); the novel *The UnSimple* [in the journal *Ukrainian Literature, Part One in Vol. 2 (2007), Part Two in Vol. 3* (2011)]; and excerpts of *FM Galicia* (in *The White Chalk of Days: The Contemporary Ukrainian Literary Series Anthology*, 2017).

Prokhasko is considered one of the best Ukrainian essayists, and he has two of the most prestigious Ukrainian prizes for essay writing: the 2020 Shevchenko National Prize for Literature and the 2019 BBC Book of the Year Prize in the category of essays.

Prokhasko lives and works in Ivano-Frankivsk, Ukraine.

## WHAT FOR, NOT WHY

Emptiness is also part of what I have been collecting. When you think about nothing, you can think about how you think about nothing. My whole life, I have been living like a true researcher. To draw a comparison with that fundamental science that became my coordinate system in the cognition of the world, I have always been discovering, gathering, classifying, systematizing, and preserving knowledge about different forms of life, about various manifestations of life. First and foremost, I have been learning how to gain the most private knowledge, or, as old innocents would say—the one I never read about.

Most probably, it all started from a childish wish to appropriate the world, to acquire and master it. In this sense, the knowledge of things, the ability to register their names, and the capability of naming the unnamed is a more reliable and complete form of possession than full-contact expansion or any other way of taking root.

Attempts at the purest possible understanding, a wish to declare one's achievements and properties, and, finally—the terminal station—a conscious desire to share, give, give back, and give over could be the next levels in the hierarchy of needs. They'd be rewarded, indeed, with an understanding that would coincide with gratitude and love. That is—storytelling.

My whole life, I have been studying life, primarily the hard way, having transformed myself into a multidisciplinary experimental testing ground. And all that only to write about it—ultimately, soon, one day. Experience for the sake of fiction became so strategic that life per se transformed: I could take its piece, as tiny as a wood chip, and use it to create fiction. However, I never staged experiments or created anything deliberately—I just never avoided what was happening, seeing it as yet another fragment of a periodic table or register or appendix to the universal code for reconstructing the unknown from the elements of the known.

My whole life, I have been studying details, textures, and nodal points through which you can draw paradoxically accurate and beautiful curves to factorize them later into spatial models of figures cobbled together from twisted continuous planes.

My whole life, minute by minute, I have been picking words, phrases, and sentences which—like a collapsed card castle—could fold up with a breath of wind into another one, almost the same but slightly different, compressing into the paragraphs of detailed description of phenomena. Thanks to that (or for the sake of that), miraculous properties have evolved: mindful vision; discernment of building blocks in large-scale constructions; the ability to distinguish one block from another; and the capability of visualizing the exact location it should take in space to dim other structural elements.

I have studied and memorized so many words, believing that this knowledge guarantees a hardly achievable fullness of love to the world. I feel sorry even to start recounting all these categories and classifications of types, destinies, materials, forms, shades, pains, experiences, emotions, assumptions, hints, passwords, vanities, thrills, movements, smells, illusions, addictions, misunderstandings, and revelations.

But here is a weird thing. I have keys to entire apartments, floors, attics, annexes, and basements—but I have never used them. Life as fiction, life for the sake of fiction, turned out to be unusable and unused in real fiction. It became a wonderful way of spending the time that defines it bearably. I have shared almost nothing. I have been left alone with my keys to the knowledge about the structure of the contemporal world—the knowledge built with my own molecules. It seems as if I implemented only one of the perfect natural strategies—to live in such a way as to leave as few traces as possible.

But imaginary fiction as a way of holding out is a fairly good method. I might as well share it.

*November 7, 2019*

## I JUST HOPE THEY WON'T NEED US

When I was a child, back in primary school, I felt that the main enchantment of Christmas Eve was its mysteriousness. It seemed to me that only a select few from a limited network of people knew that Christmas existed for real. Therefore, it had to be celebrated. As a child, I did not doubt that a holiday could not do without festive food. It was only that the Christmas dinner had to be prepared much more thoroughly. You were supposed to eat not what you enjoyed but what God or at least the Holy Family preferred. I was glad that God, who usually avoided direct instructions, relieved people of having to deliberate and devise, and provided a clear menu.

I was surprised the first few times when I tried *kutia*[8] at our relatives'. It tasted different. It was then that I seriously considered the probability of all kinds of heresies, protestantisms, and denominations. Seemingly, decent people allowed themselves to stray, more or less, from God's mandatory recipe, so what could you say about things much less palpable and calculated?

I imagined Holy Supper as a straightforward pre-order. In case someone does not let Them in again, and

---

8 Kutia is a ceremonial grain dish with sweet gravy traditionally served by Eastern Orthodox Christians and Byzantine Catholic Christians.

They ask us to host them overnight. Then we could serve the food that God explicitly wished for. The treat They wanted to get.

I imagined Christmas dinner as a certain expectation. The readiness to become a host. A small backing for Pantocrator[9] in His risky earthly journey. They never visited us in the flesh, but it did not make me sad or frustrated. It was the other way around. It meant that things were all right. The network was not full of holes. Someone let Them in. Someone hosted Them. And now Joseph and Mary (it is funny that I named them in that particular order, apparently, influenced by a pattern of childhood experience when a man, a father, was supposed to make the family safe and handle all kinds of trouble) were somewhere nearby enjoying *varenyky*[10], *borscht*[11], fish, beans, and kutia, washing it all down with *uzvar*[12] made from special plums, under the first and all other stars, by a three-light candelabrum painted in three colors, green, yellow, and brown.

The underground atmosphere reinforced my childhood feelings, making them an absolute constant. I

---

9 A title of Christ represented as the ruler of the universe, especially in Byzantine church decoration.

10 Varenyky are one of the main Ukrainian national dishes. They are made from fresh dough and a variety of fillings, such as meat, potatoes, mushrooms, vegetables, fruits, cheese, and other ingredients.

11 Borscht is the main Ukrainian national dish. It is a sour soup made with red beetroots as one of the main ingredients, which give the dish its distinctive red color. Depending on the region, ingredients for borscht and type of serving vary (mushrooms, beans, red pepper; green borscht, cold borscht).

12 Uzvar is a national Ukrainian beverage, cooked with dried fruits and berries.

was overcome with excitement, and it never occurred to me that with electric lights off, the reflections of candles on the large curtained window overlooking the main street screamed to outsiders about a mystery disclosed.

As a teenager, I was occupied with other things. I thought how intricate the script was of the last few hours of a fetus yet to be born, The One who knew everything and who would not be delivered at a palace or another decent establishment. What would have happened to us but for a barn? What kind of *vertep*[13], carols, festive dinners, and houses with their just-in-case preparations would we have had?

Only once in my life did I not prepare the dinner that would suit Them. There were no ingredients, no conditions, nobody to share it with. No, I am lying. There was somebody. My driver was right there next to me—an uneducated Muslim, but still. He was ready for anything. And I told him everything. He joined the network.

But it was freezing cold and empty all around us. A large black-and-white meadow. A frozen ironclad warship—a good man would never send his dog into it. Frozen biscuits. Some hard tea. Three non-filter cigarettes for the two of us and another five days ahead. However, one of the stations could catch Luxembourg radio. However, people in that country were living in another temporal dimension, and in early January, just like all the uninitiated, said nothing about the forthcoming birth.

I hoped very much that the state of the world was

---

13 Vertep is the Ukrainian tradition of the nativity story presented using a puppet theater.

better than almost two thousand years ago. Most probably, that night, we were not going to be useful—fortunately. But, I said to my only Muslim, should anyone knock on the frozen armor, should a suspicious man and woman appear out of nowhere, then despite the prohibitions of our absurd restricted access facility, we would let them in. Without asking for a password; putting the guns down. After all, we still had cookies, strong tea, and cigarettes. And we could cover Them with inflatable life jackets. To make water for the woman in labor, we could melt snow with our own bodies.

*January 6, 2022*

## LIVING WITH A NATURAL DISASTER

For all things in the world are connected. And no element can function without interacting with others. And therefore, comparisons in the area of botanical geography—just like any other selective comparisons— do not reduce comprehension of human communities to helpless naturalism. Botanical geography is teaching about habitats, limiting factors, expansion, ecological niche, interspecific competition on a certain territory, indigenous and introduced species, symbiosis, and mutual displacement.

Having lived in the same place for half a century, I believe even more in naturalistic analogies and metaphors, which—according to the laws of universal understanding of systems—can somehow explain what happens around me.

For the past fifty years or, given the historical continuity, even longer, I have been feeling like a plant that has to fight for its living space not so much caring about the future of its species but so as not to wither all alone, with a permanent sense of how its biotope diversifies due to the slow, relentless invasion of another species.

This is a given. This is botanical geography.

The geography is such that our habitat neighbors

on Russians. The given is such that they are expansive. So, they are not only around—they have been here for a long while. Their limiting neighborhood, their penetration into new territories is ultimately about something much more significant than the warmth, humidity, salinity, and composition of our soils. We co-exist with an aggressive species that can adapt to any conditions and spread even to locations that have already been taken—they expand because they can destroy the conditions they find themselves in, degrade them to fit their needs, and regenerate the species adapted to specific habitats.

Nearby neighborhoods and proximity to Russians are unchangeable factors. No climate change can transform the destiny of the Ukrainian people. It always happens that something that seemingly does not let you live a normal life is, in fact, the most genuine life, its fullest manifestation. This is how the co-existence of Ukrainians and Russians should be viewed. Ukrainians—as long as they are true to themselves—will never be able to live a normal life, withstanding the Russian factor. But perhaps it is this eternal confrontation, this continuous pressure that Ukrainians have to withstand that makes their life full and complete—a genuine, consciously chosen existence.

In this moment of realization, stoicism can help. It might well qualify as our national ideology. The Russian factor cannot be changed—we can only change our attitude toward it. Recognize that the other side will never back down. Consequently, in a situation like this, we cannot compare ourselves with people whose destiny is unlike ours. We must live our life, accepting that its meaning is not in the achievement of some heavenly expectations and standards (or purgatory), but in the intense and fascinating hell of self-preservation, self-determination, and resistance to the expansion in which we play a unique and difficult role as Russia's neighbor. Neither its disappearance, nor displacement, nor even neutralization, complete liberation, or escape are possible. The neighbor is already among us.

It will dissolve the weaker ones. It will burn everyone without exception. The fire will spare you only if you don't regret anything destined to become unattainable and lost for you as Russia's neighbor. It is a significant game, this one. It transforms physics into ethics.

*November 29, 2018*

*Translated from Ukrainian by Hanna Leliv*

Hanna Leliv lives in Lviv, Ukraine, where she works as a freelance translator and runs literary translation workshops at the Ukrainian Catholic University. She was a Fulbright fellow at the University of Iowa's Literary Translation MFA program and mentee at the Emerging Translators Mentorship Program run by the UK National Centre for Writing. Her translations of contemporary Ukrainian literature into English have appeared in *Asymptote*, *BOMB*, *Washington Square Review*, *The Adirondack Review*, *The Puritan*, and elsewhere. In 2022, *Stalking the Atomic City: Life Among the Decadent and the Depraved of Chornobyl*, a non-fiction book by Markiyan Kamysh, was published in her English translation by Astra House.

# SERHIY
# ZHADAN

A poet, fiction writer, essayist, and translator (b. 1974 Luhansk Region), Zhadan is the most popular poet of the post-independence generation in Ukraine. He is the author of twelve books of poetry and seven novels that have earned him numerous national and international awards, including the Derek Walcott Prize for Poetry (USA, 2021) and the 2022 Peace Prize of the German Book Trade and the EBRD Literature Prize for his novel *The Orphanage*. Zhadan's books have been translated into many languages. The English translations of Zhadan's work include *Depeche Mode* (Glagoslav Publications, 2013), *Voroshilovgrad* (Deep Vellum Publishing, 2016), *The Orphanage* (Yale University Press, 2020) as well as the collection of short stories and poems *Mesopotamia* (Yale University Press, 2018), the collection of selected poems *What We Live For/What We Die For* (Yale University Press, 2019), and the drama *A Harvest Truce* (Harvard University Press, forthcoming in 2022).

In addition to writing, Zhadan has translated poems by Bertolt Brecht, Paul Celan, and Charles Bukowski into Ukrainian. He is the frontman for the band Zhadan and the Dogs, and has collaborated on theatre and performance projects with Yara Arts Group (New York) since 2002.

The theme of Ukraine's East and its struggle with a Soviet past has shaped Zhadan's creative landscape. Starting from 2014, his poetry shows the power of the word in a time of war. Since the war began in 2014, Zhadan has emerged as an iconic voice of a free Ukraine. In 2022, the Committee for Literary Studies of the Polish Academy of Sciences proposed Zhadan for the Nobel Prize for Literature.

Zhadan lives in Kharkiv, where he helps organize humanitarian aid for civilians and military.

\*\*\*

All eternity lies ahead.
There's time to talk about important things.
Sun rays bursting through the airy fabric.
Finally he is coming home.
How long was he gone? she asks.
No time to re-read letters written long ago.
No time for hesitation or doubt.
Time emerges out of short breaths,
breathless words, naked
shoulder blades, time is joy and wonder.

He tells her about important things,
things that strengthen her shoulders
and make her knees ring.
Time is silence and breath,
the movement of planets, her gestures as she fixes her hair.

Time for insight and fatigue will come,
as will time for hesitation.
But now is not the time to let go of
important things,
not the time to doubt the truth of this light.
There's a time to love and be silent,
There's time to love and listen,
to return, believe and love.

All of eternity awaits.
The earth circles the sun.

The sea retreats from the corridors at night.
Heavy men's shoes lay near the bed,
like boats, tossed ashore
after a long voyage.

First published in Ukrainian in *2018* (*Antenna* by Meridian Czernowitz). Permission to reproduce the works granted by German publisher Suhrkamp Verlag.

\*\*\*

Someone touches your arm,
breaking all the rules.
Summer ends.
Honeycombs
heavy and dark, like icons.

Only later will the fear pass of
a startling handshake in the street.
Children grow up in eastern cities,
believing in the sun, like scripture.

The Quiet East,
the dark soil
of your fields is like a mourning dress.
Whose loses and loneliness
Gave birth to all of us here?

Each scribe and rebel
sprung to life here
with one religion – the feeling that
later someone will avenge them.

The edges are built into the foundation
of this spacious building.
So much summer.
So much weight.
Again and again

First published in Ukrainian in *2020* (*List of Ships* by
Meridian Czernowitz).

\*\*\*

From now on there's so much amazement
among poets and travelers
as winter's army cadences
roll over the mainland.

These shores, used to suffering,
are bound by laws and legends,
sunken sailors, underwater flowers
that come apart as sad petals.

The first word is the first light
one day a shadow will cross each shutter.
The army readies chains and saddles
accepting death for justice and loyalty.

I have a warm home and blankets for the road,
divine inspiration, colds and stigmata;
I've enough stories
to brave through winter,

about defectors and psychopaths,
about late autumn – those who believe that faith alone
brings salvation.
Everything will change before the first snowfall.
Everything will change before morning.
What you always knew and what you finally learned,
Signals, warnings and interference.
Winter appears like a book of poems
No one will ever publish.

First published in Ukrainian in *2021* (*Psalm of Aviation* by
Meridian Czernowitz)

*Translated from Ukrainian by Virlana Tkacz and Wanda Phipps*

Virlana Tkacz heads the Yara Arts Group and has directed almost forty original shows at La MaMa Experimental Theatre Club in New York, as well as at venues in Kyiv, Lviv, Kharkiv, Bishkek, Ulaanbaatar, and Ulan Ude. She has received a National Endowment of the Arts Poetry Translation Fellowship for her translations with Wanda Phipps.

Wanda Phipps is the author of the books *Mind Honey*, *Field of Wanting: Poems of Desire*, and *Wake-Up Calls: 66 Morning Poems*. She received a New York Foundation for the Arts Poetry Fellowship. Her poems have appeared in over one-hundred literary magazines and numerous anthologies.

Virlana Tkacz and Wanda Phipps have received the AGNI Poetry Translation Prize, the National Theatre Translation Fund Award, and thirteen translation grants from the New York State Council on the Arts. *What We Live For, What We Die For: Selected Poems* by Serhiy Zhadan, with translations by Virlana Tkacz and Wanda Phipps, was published by Yale University Press in 2019. Their translations have also appeared in many literary journals and anthologies, and are integral to the theatre pieces created by Yara Arts Group.

# LYUBKO
# DERESH

One of the most well-known Ukrainian contemporary writers (b. 1974, Lviv region), Deresh, by the time he was eighteen, published two novels—*Cult* and *Worshiping the Lizard*—and achieved acclaim as a writer. Deresh is now an author of ten books of prose, two children's books, and a number of essays. For his style and popularity among readers, especially teenagers, the media have proclaimed Deresh the Ukrainian Stephen King. His works have been translated into several European languages.

His novels featured teenage protagonists and described significant stories from their lives. Unlike prior generations, his young characters, who grow up in free Ukraine, are unburdened by a Soviet past. In order to truthfully show the life of the characters, the author uses common modern slang and sometimes swear words. The characters of Deresh's novels have constantly been searching for the meaning of their earthly existence, as well as the border between worlds, between material and immaterial, and dream and reality.

Deresh currently resides and works in Kyiv, Ukraine.

## IN THE TUILERIES GARDENS

*If you are the amber mare*
*I am the road of blood*

– Octavio Paz

Late at night, Slim and Jesus wandered through Podil to the metro on their way home from rehearsal. It was late autumn and the puddles in the potholes on the path to the Taras Shevchenko station, choppily lit up by the streetlamps, were already covered with a crunchy layer of frost. The guys walked in silence, still thinking about the conversation at the end of the band meeting. After the concert on Monday, Alice, their so-to-speak manager, proposed they tour Ukraine in December. And today, although Alice wasn't there—on Wednesday evenings she went to her film directing class—they spent half the rehearsal arguing if it was worth going on tour right before exams. Slim tried to convince everyone that right now the idea was a real stretch. Both in how much it would cost and how much hassle it would be—and were they even ready for it anyway? But the real reason he wasn't burning with desire to go on tour was something totally different. Walking beside Jesus, Slim thought about their discussion and from time to time nervously shifted his guitar case from one shoulder to the other and, gripping a cigarette in his numb fingers, took a short, tense drag. Jesus, who'd been completely silent all this time, finally giggled and asked Slim from under his ridiculous knitted hat:

"It's because of Alice you don't want to go, right?"

Slim was always very secretive about his personal life and if he opened up to anyone about it then probably it would be Nazik, his friend of many years.

"What? No, what does Alice have to do with anything?" Slim shook his head, not wishing to share with Jesus the details of his relationship with their manager. Although, no doubt, it was impossible not to notice that there was something between them.

"I mean, she, like, spent the night at your place after the concert, right?" Jesus raised one eyebrow in that way he had. Of course, it would have been hard not to remember that moment, because on Monday night the idea of the tour seemed perfectly fine to Slim, but by Tuesday morning he'd written in their chat that, most likely, he wouldn't go anywhere. Slim was the band's lead singer and his refusal to go meant the tour couldn't happen at all. On Monday (just the day before yesterday, but it seemed like a lifetime ago) they gave a concert at one of the rock clubs in Obolon, after which they all went over to Slim's place to celebrate their first success. Slim lived by himself in a large apartment right next to the Botanical Gardens behind the University metro. Animated by their successful performance and warmed by several martinis, Alice proposed they go on tour; she would be the organizer.

"Well, sure," Slim nodded. "But, like, nothing

happened."

Jesus didn't say anything, just waited to hear more. Slim kept quiet too, recalling with some pain that their martini party on Monday had ended with Alice announcing to everybody that she was spending the night here, with her "darling Slim," because her parents' house was complete trash.

When the rest of the band left after the sudden revelation (as the boys mentally named it, and Slim himself mentally named it) of his and Alice's intimate relations, the two of them went to the store for whiskey and salted peanuts. Slim's parents, who were divorced and lived separately, didn't worry too much about their youngest son's success. But sometimes they gave him large sums of money to live on, as though compensating for their lack of attention. Certain he knew where all this was headed, Slim pretended he'd forgotten to buy cigarettes (although he still had some left) and, leaving the unbelievably drunk and noisy Alice in her unbuttoned sleazy leather jacket to wait by the supermarket, went back to the cashier to buy a pack of condoms. He was certain that things were fatefully leading to his ordination from boy to man. Slim was both afraid and excited by this.

His relationship with Alice had been unclear from the beginning. Slim had fallen for the crazy gleam in her dark eyes and her childish and touchingly innocent face practically at first sight, when Alice would either come close to him, warming him with her attention and giving him hope, or even certainty, that they would get together, or she would suddenly turn into an icicle again—an embittered, superior, inaccessible, incredibly narcissistic egotist with a set of devastating words that she seemed to have saved all her life just to criticize Slim's singing. Just that summer, during the Atlas Weekend rock festival where the band was playing, Alice drank too much and spent a whole night French kissing him next to the stage. After this, Slim realized he was completely crazy about her. Alice's coldness the very next day threw rocks on his hopes that their relationship would be clear. Were they together or not? Did she need him? Would she ever be able to say how she felt about him without smirking and hiding behind her jokes and tricks?

"You mean, nothing at all?" Jesus asked, and Slim felt him literally drag each word out of him. But there was something about Jesus that didn't allow Slim to just clam up and cut off the conversation. In fact, there was something in Jesus' simple directness that Slim even liked.

"Like, we just lay next to each other, that's it." Slim said guardedly, avoiding his eyes. Then he couldn't resist and added: "Long story short, she was, like, plastered and crashed on the bed in her jeans and sweater."

"That's it?" Jesus repeated with good-natured amusement. An experienced and knowing smile played on his lips.

"I mean, yeah." Slim's shoulders sank; his eyes looked straight ahead, full of pain. They could already see the steps to the Taras Shevchenko metro station. "I tried to make a move on her but she only snorted like a horse and accidentally stuck a finger in my eye."

Jesus burst out laughing (he always laughed at random times) and unexpectedly cheered Slim up too.

"Want me to tell you how I tricked an underage

girl one time?" Jesus suddenly said.

"An underage girl?" Slim asked with some disapproval.

"It was back in the summer, right?" Jesus happily shrugged.

"Well, sure," Slim nodded.

"Right before exams. Long story, I picked up a little girl, a slut. She'd be in 8th grade now, maybe 9th."

"No way."

"Serious." Jesus gave Slim a cheerful and excited wink from under his hat. "Long story, I'm walking near the Lisova metro and right in front of me is a flock of these little girls—no way to get around them. And I hear, like, one of them saying that some guy, like, approached her and is like, 'hey girl, come with me, suck me off and I'll give you, like, twenty hryvnias.' So she's like, 'No way I'll suck you off for twenty hryvnias, you'll only get a hand job.' I dig around in my pocket and I happen to have twenty hryvnias. So I'm like, 'Hey girl, listen, I got a twenty in my pocket. Come on, I'll buy you an ice cream.' Her friends left and the girl and me went off together. She says, 'let's go behind this building, I'll do everything to you.' I'm like, 'no way, there's people there. Come on, there's a building near here with a roof—no one'll see us there.' And, long story, we went to the next building where you could get onto the roof."

"Holy crap." Slim shook his head at Jesus, not quite disapproving and not quite approving.

"I know, right?" Jesus' eyes shone at the memory. "So we go up to the roof and I'm shitting myself thinking now we'll get caught, and I can see she's nervous too. When we get to the roof we see the sunset over Lisovyi Park. It's so hot, there's pollen from the poplars everywhere, all that crap. From the 9th floor we can see like the whole neighborhood—clear to Victory Park. And, long story, I feel really bad that I dragged her there."

"So what'd you do?" Now Slim was getting curious.

Jesus tried to look serious, but a smile was playing at the corners of his mouth.

"Long story, I let her listen to my iPod. Whitesnake, I think. I asked what she listens to—she has no clue about music, right? So I, like, give her one earphone and listen with the other myself. We each had a cig, listened to a couple of tracks, then went back down."

"That's it?" Disappointed, Slim raised his brows.

"We saw the sunset," Jesus reminded him. "She admitted she made it all up for her girlfriends that she did everything with boys and asked me not to tell anybody. But she took the twenty hryvnias. Cool girl, really nice…"

"That's it?" Slim asked again, even more sarcastically.

"Well, yeah," nodded Jesus. He paused. "Well, I like asked if I could kiss her, and we sucked face a while. You never know how it'll be with girls."

They got on the metro and after a few stops they parted. Slim had to go only three stops, while Jesus needed to go all the way to Lisova.

"Touring Ukraine is a legit idea," he said to Slim as he left. "Write me if you change your mind. We'll pick up some sluts somewhere…"

Although he spoke with complete seriousness, Jesus' eyes gleamed slyly.

"Ok," grumbled Slim, avoiding his eyes.

**********

It was almost ten-thirty when Slim got home. The apartment his parents had given him was dark and empty. It had remained unfinished for eleven years: huge, unfurnished, with bare walls and a fine oak floor that had never been stained in all that time—no one had had time for it. The only inhabited corners were the kitchen, the shower and Slim's nook, where he had a mattress, a laptop and two large Marshall speakers. Slim entered the apartment without turning on the lights; he put his guitar case in the corner, tossed off his things and went to his room. Through the round windows with neither curtains nor blinds, lights from the streetlamps poured into the dark room that was warmed by hot radiators. Slim dropped onto his mattress, shoving a pillow under his head that still carried the smell of Alice's perfume. Taking out his smartphone, he spent a long time surfing social media; he didn't dare write to Alice—but then for some reason decided to call her.

Alice picked up almost immediately.

"Hello?" He heard an achingly familiar voice. She was talking with her mouth full. Her voice was businesslike, no note of the intimacy Slim's heart so needed at that moment.

"Hi, Al," Slim answered. "Can you talk now?"

"I'm in Paris right now," she answered, still chewing something. He could hear a noise on Alice's end; loud voices were arguing.

"What do you mean you're 'in Paris'?"

"Just what I said." She swallowed something and took a large sip of some hot drink before continuing. "I bought a ticket this morning and was already at Charles de Gaulle by lunch. Right now I'm sitting in the Tuileries, eating a baguette and drinking coffee."

"You're messing with me," Slim said in confusion. He sat up on the mattress and scratched his head thoughtfully. He could hear cursing in the background that definitely didn't sound French. Slim looked anxiously out the window at the overcast Kyiv sky lit by streetlamps. "You mean your folks are fighting again?"

Alice's parents were highly problematic. The latest Alice had told him was that her mom in a drunken fit had tried to break down the door to the bathroom where her dad was hiding.

"No, fuck you!" A woman's voice could be heard in the receiver, then a thud as some heavy piece of furniture fell over, then someone's drunken whining.

"No," Alice said in a calm, detached voice. "Those are just some bums on the other bank of the Seine."

"Got it," Slim said, and lay back on the pillow. His eyes stared at the car headlights flitting across the ceiling. "So how are you? How's the weather in Paris?"

"Crappy," Alice said curtly, slurping her coffee again. "Only good for ducks. It's warmer than in Kyiv. Just the wind is strong. What's up, Slim? Make it fast, my roaming's on."

There was another noise on her end and Alice suddenly put her phone down and slammed the door a few times. She yelled somewhere down the corridor: "Hey, keep it down out there!"

The shouting grew a little louder but when Alisa slammed the door behind her, the drunken lament died down again.

"Nothing much, really...," Slim managed to say. "Just wanted to say what a cool idea it was about the tour. I think we should go."

"Great," said Alice expressionlessly. Slim got the impression that if he hadn't agreed to go she would have easily found a replacement for him.

They were silent for a bit.

"Listen, can I sit next to you?" Slim suddenly asked. "We can listen to my phone together."

"Sure, sit down," Alice replied after a pause. He could hear she was intrigued.

Slim sat beside Alice on the cold metal chair right next to the stone side of a large round birdbath. Alice, bundled like a sparrow in her pea coat and scarf, sat next to him. She tried not to look at him, but Slim thought he could pick up a glimmer of gratitude in the looks she stole at him from time to time in the dark garden.

"Here," Slim handed Alice an earphone and put the other in his ear. He put on some jazz from the playlist on his phone. The bassist slowly plucking his strings. The lonely trumpeter in the distance. *If you are the amber mare, I am the road of blood.*

"Don't give them so much bread," he said, taking the baguette from Alice and breaking off a good-sized chunk for himself.

"Now listen, Slim—don't interfere. These are my ducks, I can do what I want." A small but warm and touching smile suddenly appeared on Alice's face—the first in long months of Slim's hapless attempts to get some sign of affection from her.

"They aren't yours," he objected. "They're for everyone."

Alice didn't know what to say to that but in the darkness Slim could clearly see her happily tuck her chin into the thick scarf that smelled of cigarettes and her girlish perfume. Far away in the sky above the Louvre a warm, agitated Parisian wind chased clouds lit up by the lights of the great city. The bare branches in the deserted Tuileries Gardens rustled mysteriously and a bit alarmingly. Slim sat next to Alice on a chair that hadn't been put away for the night, drinking in the smell of her perfume and coffee. From time to time he tossed a bit of the still-warm baguette to the ducks who, the little dopes, happily ruffled up their backs and pecked at the mirror of black water in the dark. Slim smiled at Alice who, leaning her feet on the edge of the tub, wrapped her arms around herself and tried not to pay attention to the shouts and noise coming from the other side of the Seine. At first he wanted to say something meaningful but then stopped himself: it wasn't worth it. Everything was fine just as it was.

*2021*

LYUBKO DERESH

*Translated from Ukrainian by Catherine O'Neil*

Catherine O'Neil is a literary scholar and professor of Russian language and culture at the United States Naval Academy. She received her PhD from the University of Chicago and her MA from the University of Toronto. She works on Russian, Ukrainian and Polish literature. She is currently translating two novels by Ukrainian writer Alexei Nikitin: *Victory Park* and *The Face of Fire*.

# PAVLO
# KOROBCHUK

Ukrainian poet, novelist, musician, and journalist (b. 1984, Lutsk), Korobchuk is the author of six books of poetry and three books of prose. Winner of about twenty literary prizes, he is considered one of the leaders of the aughts poetry generation. He has performed more than twenty musical performances as an actor and poetry reader on Amy Winehouse's work with the band The Velvet Sun. Korobchuk is engaged in literary criticism and has published more than thirty critical reviews of works of modern Ukrainian literature in media.

In his work, he redefines the history of Ukraine's independence, and through the characters of his books, he shows the importance of the struggle for personal independence. His recent poems are mostly related to the theme of war. There are various complex topics: from war stories with a plot to existential poetic reflections or purely figurative, formal interpretations. But even his recent poetry is not devoid of sentimental motifs, themes of love, and hope.

He lives in Kyiv, Ukraine.

PAVLO KOROBCHUK

## LETTER FROM A SAILOR TO HIS DAUGHTER

Let my voice say nothing to you.
You simply listen to it, as if it were the sound of the surf.
Seas, great forces, allow us to pray with joy.
Indeed, lesser the mass of our bodies,
        lesser the mass of our pain.

My voice, for a long time, in the sense of another
        listening, hasn't had support.
All that was said rarely, swarmed in coarse strokes within.
After all, to communicate with someone is like unto hiring
        a servant.
It happens in good word, but sometimes in evil tongues.

Although it is no need to speak to be understood.
After all, there may be enough fingers at the piano.
And thus, the boats transform into woodwork.
And thus, the jellyfish become the ocean.

That's what I've witnessed in many long years of absence.
Among agonies toward death, in captivity among slaves.
Seems like it would drive me into a stupor and stiffen me.
Just let it go with me to the bottom,
        like chests in leaky ships.

I am writing you from the shore, I'm attaching a palm
leaf to the text.
From here it is most clear, that the Earth is round,
        more precisely – an arena.

105

# LETTER FROM A SAILOR TO HIS DAUGHTER

On this unpeopled island, everything is like pills;
which have expired and feel in your body
       as if your lease ran out.

I don't long for my youth – because she is another.
I don't shun removed tatters – because he was dressed in
       every one of them.
In place of youthful sweat comes tactile chemistry.
The blood takes on the flavor of blackberries.

*2013*

## LIVE LIKE FINGERS ON A SHEET OF PAPER

Live simple. Peacefully. Live just as you love.
Love just as you live.
Live with hugs and in hugs, in warmth and disturbance.
Live easily.
Live being thanks to yesterday and for the tomorrow
        that you yourself call everything.
Live like the calligraphy of a bird taking wing.
Like a decorated pen.

Like fingers on a sheet, that transform the universe
        into origami.
Like a cluster of alveoli that change the tone of winter air.
Live with quiet, Live in harmony with the waves, the sea,
        and the shore.
Live like you were placing a feather at the edge of infinity.
Live in name.

Rye or wheat. Fresh or with hardened crust.
It isn't important.
Whether from the murk or the tops of the trees.
There is no difference.
Live like you've decided when it will be dawn and when
        there will be a downpour.
Like just as if the reaches of space begin with your pupil.

Keys from the games on which the spine is straightened
        and smoothen protrusions.

Rhythms that filigree repeat mistily the lines
      of mountain ranges.
Live in melodies, hear the strings' meridian,
      dreams and illusions.
Live in the way that you sometimes curse yourself for
      never having managed.

Live gratefully for the thought of those
      who haven't yet been born.
Gratefully for those soon to be present;
grateful for the idea of what's next.
Like a dog, that senses that someone close will open
      the door.
Like a boy who succeeded in keeping his balance
      by cranking the pedals.

*2020*

## SKY OVER A SANDALWOOD TREE

—When did you move to this city?
—During the last summer,
 when a single ray of light crossed
from this point to that point.

—When did you give birth to children?
—As the sun crossed the galaxy,
and baked my pale face,
and tore the dark matter into shreds.

—When did peace settle upon your house?
—When the tails of comets,
in the field of view of the largest telescopes,
have shifted by only a millimeter.

—When do you find time to weave a braid?
—I don't find time, my fingers just work,
while I sleep in bed, amidst the cosmos,
wrapped in a warm blanket of gravitation.

—Where are you moving to? What will happen to you
next?
—For a million years the trajectory of the planet
Has guided me through the sky over a sandalwood tree,
standing above this fountain where coins are thrown.

*2020*

## SISTER

See, in my pupils, there are swallows and daisies.
See, in my lungs, the field sways in the wind.
In all of the other native creatures
       yet there are very few letters.

Sister, this has never happened to you in the light.
Your name was never whispered or spoken
Just as no one said: "run," "laugh," or "oak woods."

You would stand beside me, with it all in your lungs and
       pupils,
And reality would twinkle, like expensive souvenirs:
"the way," "to talk," "to walk," "memories," "here,"
       "trust."

I wouldn't have known what to say,
I would be chattering the whole time.
I would be made to quickly remember a few decades.
Those, where you were not – treats and losses.

We would have overcome all our troubles.
You are the immanence of wise,
       accurate and correct deeds.
We would walk side by side, step by step.

The word "sister" will not be delicate and soft,
No matter how many silkworms weave the words
       of eternity,

# SISTER

Evening removes the earrings,
            puts them in the dark drawer.

See, in my pupils, there are swallows and daisies.
See, everything is perfect; the field sways in the wind.
It's just that I'll never know the letters of your name.

*2019*

PAVLO KOROBCHUK

*Translated from Ukrainian by Charles Bonds*

Charles Bonds holds a doctorate in history from Indiana University. He is the Vice-President of Art and Soul of Ukraine, an organization that supports artists, art therapy, and beautification projects in Ukraine. He teaches English in Lviv, writes poetry and prose, volunteers, and paints digitally and on canvas.

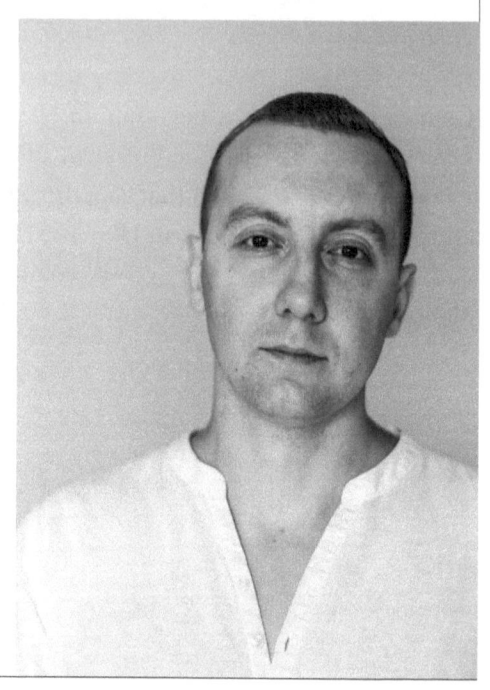

# STANISLAV
# ASEYEV

A journalist and writer (b. Donetsk,1989), Aseyev is an author of philosophical and surrealistic prose and poems, which he wrote predominantly in Russian. After the beginning of the Russian–Ukrainian war, he remained in Donetsk in order to describe the reality surrounding him objectively while anonymously working with many leading Ukrainian media under the pseudonym Stanislav Vasin. In June 2017, he was arrested by so-called Donetsk People's Republic (DPR) militants and thrown into Izolyatsia prison—a modern-day concentration camp—where he was beaten and tortured. Later, in his collection *In Isolation: Dispatches from Occupied Donbas* (translated into English by Lidia Wolanskyj for Harvard Library of Ukrainian Literature, 2022), he describes the early period of the Russian military aggression in Ukraine's east from 2015–2017. In December 2019, he was returned to Ukraine as a result of a prisoner exchange after two years imprisoned in the concentration camp. The Ukrainian Center for Civil Liberties, which received The Nobel Peace Prize 2022, was involved in the advocacy campaign #FreeAseyev. The campaign #PrisonersVoice in support of Ukrainian political prisoners in Russia and in the Russian-occupied territories of Ukraine continues to this day.

Aseyev wrote the documentary book *The Torture Camp on Paradise Street*, the most important evidence of the atrocities of the DPR militants in the prisons under their control. The book has been translated into many languages, including English by Zenia Tompkins and Nina Murray (Old Lion Publishing, 2021). He is actively engaged in human rights and educational activities. Aseyev's early literary texts are philosophical, absurd, and strange. His contemporary works are evidence of life against the backdrop of war, with all its cruelties, pain, disappointment, heroism, and courage, recorded with scrupulous accuracy.

He lives and works in Kyiv, Ukraine.

## PRUNUS ARMENIACA

My Crimean diary. No mistakes, no revisions. If a diary is basically the past, then I would start mine with an apricot. Crimea preceded it all. It came before the French Foreign Legion and Marx, before the strange feelings toward women and the women themselves, even before the Russians, though back then, we were probably Russian ourselves. It preceded everything, like a kind of Holy Spirit, darting this way and that over the fathomless ocean, with a mischievous smile on its face. Just as I had always associated Leningrad with a box of chocolates and St. Petersburg with a horse-drawn carriage, Crimea to me was an apricot. And we're not talking about an abstract apricot either, but rather a very specific apricot which only two people on Earth had the honour of contemplating.

When my father got my mother and me out of Donetsk and into Makiivka, he sketched a straight line— the first in a simple triangle. Donetsk–Makiivka–Maiske formed the three dimensions of my entire childhood. For nine months of the year, I filled my lungs with Makiivka's air, and then spent the summer under a cupola of big southern stars. Eden's virgin land, unscarred by coal-mining refuse. A million fields of corn, a bike as your main mode of transport. It penetrated your eye sockets and flushed out the slag heaps.

As my train approached the Sivash, I always worried that I'd fall asleep and "wouldn't miss it." That's how everyone used to speak back then—adding a negative where it wasn't required. That's exactly how the broken Russian of the grey mining districts infiltrated the Crimean steppes. But no sooner had you stuck your head out of the carriage, than it all instantly melted away; compared to the smog of Donetsk, the air here was like a luxury item that should have been sold alongside the buckets of fruit and whole melons. But the people here didn't charge a penny for it for some reason. That's how I would find myself transported to the other world.

I'm not joking when I refer to Eden—Maiske had no more people than the original Garden. It was surrounded on all sides by never-ending seas of fields, with fields beyond and more fields beyond those. The hamlet sat like a glittering pearl in the middle of the virgin steppe. There was a subtle parallel with Donbas here, since infinity and the steppe are one and the same. That said, the silence and gentle breeze of Maiske did have a southerly accent to them.

I swear to God, there really was hardly a soul there. The heat, dry hay and massive bushes of dill growing in the vegetable garden—those were the only inhabitants of the surrounding steppes. In terms of entertainment, there was: throwing rocks at passing freight trains to elicit a tiny shower of sparks, and racing your bike after a tractor hauling a trailer of fresh hay. When you pedal as fast as you can but still never succeed in getting closer than a meter away from that moving target. The former is fun, the latter—dangerous. Now, the one thing you really couldn't do was die of hunger—there was always something to munch on growing nearby. Black cherries, sour cherries, raspberries, fluffy grass, dry from the stem up, standing motionless in the heat. With that, and the braying of the mule in the mornings, our surrounding landscapes were complete.

I remember once sitting in a cherry tree enveloped in the exhaust fumes of a tractor, eating cherries, and then feeling sick all night. I also remember my brother occasionally selling a bucket of strawberries right off the train platform, for 20 hryvni; that would be a grave error these days. My brother is now in Odessa, and I have a view of a shell that's sticking out of the ground right outside my window.

The city is at any point an amorphous edition of itself. It self-publishes everything—clothes, faces, careers, all come off the same press, from the same "Bolshevik Woman" factory. Crimea didn't have editions. You couldn't really take harvesting bucketfuls of courgettes too seriously. Simplicity and the smell of manure were here long before people started barbecuing sausages and blowing up pylons, and I suspect they will still be here long afterwards. The only hint of politics in Maiske was the old collective farm. Lenin never could compete with the mill and Marxism gave way to a trailer full of wheat. The latter was, by the way, something akin to a salary, when we would have half a dozen sacks of it stored in our bedroom. Out in the fields, the spirit of collectivism ceased to exist and instead the gentle flame of the personal would flicker, with an intimacy usually reserved for two. Those two people are His temple and His high priests also. Everything was different in Crimea, even when it bored you sick. This "otherness" could barely be contained by language. It writhed and slithered across it, squirming and convulsing, catching itself on the suffixes and word endings until it finally broke off, mangled, to fall into the high Crimean grass. That was perhaps one of the few local cliches—we had to admit that the most important things had to remain unspoken. But then isn't every orator up on a stage a liar in one way or another?

This one time, my brother and I went to our *dacha*[14] in Maiske to take stock of the fruit crop. The trees stood barren: their green leaves trembled in the gentle breeze, the road ahead stretched more or less to eternity and the ground had dried up under the bright rays of the sun. Yet suddenly, a beautiful apricot presented itself; it was growing right out of a bare tree trunk. It was massive and resembled a large snail (that was going yellow for some reason), that had attached itself onto the tree. That apricot was a treasure. There was no harvest, not a single tree had borne fruit, apart from this one. With an air of careful reverence, my brother plucked the apricot from the trunk and split it in two. Juicy, massive, and most importantly— bright orange; it still occasionally surfaces in my mind's dull eye like the rising sun, causing me to furrow my brow.

As soon as the Russians marched into Crimea, the apricot was no more. Of course, our old house didn't go anywhere and that tree may still be standing where it always

---

14 Summer cottage.

stood. Who knows, mightn't someone encounter something similar to the strange miracle that we experienced, perhaps even the exact same thing? Perhaps, another one of those snails or a magical brooch, whatever tickles their fancy. But the apricot—the apricot has vanished into thin air. And this really isn't about politics, at least not about the essence of politics. In Crimea, the personal has been replaced by the collective. The roadsides now reek of newspaper lingo rather than the scent of wormwood. People had no faith in the wormwood—everyone knew it helped against fleas, whereas newspapers have yet to be believed.

Of course, the dead are universally adored. That's also the case with Crimea. And it was probably just an ordinary apricot.

*March 31–April 1, 2016*

STANISLAV ASEYEV

*Translated from Russian by Irina Steinberg*

Irina Steinberg is a London-based literary translator. She is a co-translator of Nadezhda Teffi's works *Subtly Worded and Other Stories* and *Memories: From Moscow to the Black Sea* as well as Irina Odoyevtseva's *Isolde*. She is also the translator of several short stories by Irina Odoyevtseva and Polina Zherebtsova.

# BORYS
# KHERSONSKY

A poet, publicist, essayist, translator, clinical psychologist, and psychiatrist (b.1950, Chernivtsi), Khersonsky is one of the most famous Russian-speaking poets of Ukraine, who spent most of his life in Odesa. Khersonsky was first published during Soviet times by the émigré press and distributed as a dissident and representative of the Samizdat—the movement aimed to disseminate anti-regime nonconformist literature through unofficial channels. He worked as a chair of the Kyiv Institute of Modern Psychology and Psychiatry and trained in universities in Canada and the United States, in particular, John Hopkins University. He descends from a prominent Jewish medical dynasty of the 19th century.

Khersonsky is the laureate of Ukrainian and international literary prizes, in particular, the "Bank Austria Literaris" (Austria, 2010), H.C. Artmann (Austria, 2014), and Incroci di Civiltà festival awards (Venice, 2022). He is the author of prose books and numerous poetry collections, as well as six monographs on psychology and psychiatry, including *Psychodiagnostics of Thinking*. He translated and published for the first time after Independence Sigmund Freud's *The*

*Interpretation of Dreams*. Khersonsky's poems are translated into many European languages and were illustrated by his friend, the renowned Ukrainian artist Oleksandr Roitburd.

Khersonsky's works are full of depth, surrealistic images, psychologism, opposition to totalitarian systems, multicultural contexts, and biblical codes. The topics of the search for identity and the way back home characterize all his work. His poetry, influenced by the tragedy of the Holocaust, is full of autobiographical impressions, motifs dedicated to Odesa, and the war in Ukraine. After Russia's invasion of eastern Ukraine in 2014, he returned to writing poetry in Ukrainian.

BORYS KHERSONSKY

# 1. FOREBODING

*(February 4–23, 2022)*
\*\*\*

What's the big deal for a port city
     if amphibious assault ships
enter the sea through a narrow channel—
     and moreover in a pair.
Previously galleys inhabited it, rowed by slaves,
     and waves drove them from behind
along with the wind from there.

And those who sit now tensed in uniform in the holds
are no more free than those who were shackled
     to the bench.
And from crown to heel their rage is exposed.
No day without an addition to the family, military and
     slavish.

And their conscience is no decree,
     and the very devil—no blood brother.
They have two gods in one—the captain
     and the first mate.
Who knows—perhaps tomorrow disembarking
     at the port,
and on the next day's flag, see,
     the hammer and sickle celebrate.

And the city's become a battlefield,
     and there's news from the fields,
and right at nine I don't want to look—
     the program Vremya.

# 1. FOREBODING

Who's last in the line for the mausoleum, asks the Leader,
to be received by our desiccated comrade Lenin?

And the captain looks through army binoculars—
        what's that, way over there?
What kind of city spread out on the slopes
        with no undue concerns?
The slaves are kings to themselves for today,
and the ships sail *en masse* to where
        no one yet expects their turn.

\*\*\*

Strange to think: perhaps these are the final peaceful days.
Before the face, before the snout, before the maw
        of enemies.
We remain alone. Friends are abandoning us.
Will the enemy's foot really trip over this ruse?
Does he really want to stuff his mouth with our land?
Has the land really gotten famished for blood?
Is his comrade really no wolf, but a boring mole?
The vampire's insatiable and tender, like some calf,
only it's not milk he sucks, but blood from the veins,
so they'll ask him later, *what regiment did you serve in?*
so his whole chest full of countless posthumous
        medallions.

The body rotted, a soul remained alone.
What can it do on the field of battle?
While up to the heavens—no way.
Awful to think perhaps these are the final peaceful days.

## 2. THE BEGINNING

*(February 24–28, 2022)*

\*\*\*

Well then, they showed up—didn't sit in the dust,
brought their sweetheart a posy
of tanks, helicopters, winged rockets,
told her all this is your fault,
you take this mine-grenade, here,
bitch, how dare you begrudge your older brother?

It's not some training pack of explosives.
We aren't barging in, we're triumphing—bitch,
  don't you object.
Knees apart, bloodied sheet—all the love you can expect.

We'll compel you to peace, to dinner from armored ovens.
No ordinary world, but Russian, you got it?—Russian!
Russian, I tell you again! Clothes on and get dinner ready!
So, where's your advocate? Stirring his tongue?
Of course you've dreamed your whole life of such
  a friendly one!
So he'd threaten to leave the offender with empty pockets,
call our pop a paranoic, a kleptomaniac,
and a Russian person—an alcoholic, a cad.
We came with fire. And you're meeting us with fire?
You tell us to fuck ourselves, so we'll be retired.
As they say, until we receive further orders,
places for fighting there—at the causal place, no shortage,
first we'll fly in as a squadron, then screw you
  with a rocket.

You know who I am, it's your Cain, your older brother.
So your angel's with you? We have a flying machine,
        then another.
We've hit on you with a whole archive,
        a whole TV screen,
we'll stick you with a tyrant clad in a transparent condom,
we have a red square, we'll arrange a parade right on it.

Go ahead leap up on the former fallen white stallion,
he's bloody, coated in vomit, in filth and shit.
I write "in shit," the program corrects it to "in shift."
Good night, comrades—in a dirty shroud,
in your beloved country that you've crapped out.

## 3. EXPLOSIVE WAVE
*(March 1–18, 2022)*
\*\*\*

An air-raid siren's an alarm clock for Russians.
However, there's no sleep without it either.
My poor mind is a light hid under a bushel.
No light to anyone. Moreover, no warm feelings.

There is no sleep—just drowsing and a coma.
A thought is salt that has lost its own power.
However, I'm not tight with the power of thought.
It got bogged down, but we have to walk on the floor.

They'll throw you to the ground for folks to crush
—and don't complain, for you know you were warned.
As they say, God forgives, whereas we do not judge,
as in childhood we might make the bike's pedals turn.

We turn the pedals, but we aren't riding.
Everything flies past, but we're stuck in place.
Our sins are forgiven, we'll pay for those of strangers.
All expecting an order for search and for arrest.

God frightens with retribution but consoles with wonder.
Eternal light on an empty grave. What's that to us?
Light's under a bushel, the house is dark, and salt has lost
        its power.
The world's not a stage but a circus, yet the arena's empty.
There's no sleep—just drowsing and a coma.
The air-raid alarm siren wails obstinately.
Come, nights of wartime, make yourselves at home.

\*\*\*

Lord God! What misfortune the enemies have brought
       here!
We want them to burn in hell—
       let them burn up from shame there.
The sense of guilt's darker than night.
       The outer darkness black.
And the immortal worm, arisen from the depths,
       drives a person mad.

The flame blazes up, and the worm doesn't sleep,
       Satan neighs like a horse.
Their envy boils in hellish cauldrons,
       their spite burns just like fires.

Let all nine circles spiral down to the very bottom.
How many enemies have stood up against us!
But for them all there is—a single lot.

\*\*\*

Is your hearing good enough for you
       to be able to distinguish
whose destroyer just flew by above the shingles?
What makes you shrink in the armchair,
       turning pale as chalk,
what makes you get used to war,
       with no usual tasks and talk?

It's not you the enemy aims at,
       you're less than zero for him,
small fry, nobody, nothing to call you in fact.
It's not you the rocket flies toward from the Russian
       warship,
and the warship that eats a dick, it's not your lifehack.

You're no one for them, a drop of mucus, a spot of spit.
And your grizzled head is just an empty pot.
While you share hundreds of alarms
       that thousands of brothers split.
And one by one the words of poems in your soul
       grew ripe and taut.

But will you be able to tell whose regiments
       walk outside the wall,
and why your internal vision is getting clouded?
Why for you Russian speech still remains
       most native of all,
it still lives and pulses from your birth—until right now.

And it's almost all the same whose tracks
       you follow down.

All the same, twist your neck or turn off from the road.
Your brothers and sisters have scattered to foreign towns.
And you—an eraser could rub out,
        a pen could strike through.

\*\*\*

There is somewhere to run to
        and there are reasons to flee,
but your teeth are sunk in this terrain—
        your jaw won't unclench,
and your legs are too weak for a runner's lane,
and your soul's petty demon raises his horns again—
*wait a wee bit more, till poverty, he says, I won't disturb you,*
        *don't move an inch.*

Halt that thinking, broadcast alarm over the sea,
as our folk say when things are bad—*azohen vey*,
the beach has been mined, there isn't a thing in the store,
what's good is that the sea is as blue as before,
Lent is beginning, remember the Father and Son
and the Spirit that moved upon the waters were the start
        of days.

There is somewhere to run to,
        but neither sense nor strength.
The enemy's fist threatened me at night at stupid length,
like, I'm coming, expect me, bed under your pale legs,
        or you get pissed off—

133

so touchy, dammit, it's not the gods
      who fill the chamber pots,
and the blood in you is like from drizzling autumn rain.

However, it's spring now, beginning,
      don't shiver in the wind.
There are anti-tank "hedgehogs" on the streets
      downtown,
sandbags stacked up to build barricades,
look, enemy, see—if you show up we won't be glad.
Along the shore are restaurants and high-rise masses,
if you're at loose ends—so many floors you can count.

There is somewhere to run to, but running's not practical.
In the port, a new Noah hammers together an ark.
The beasts are heading there—two of every sort,
We have to sleep wherever, but we aren't lords,
we count up our daily wage, skim fat off the broth,
demand the receipt after we pay cash in a shop.

Runners' lanes are now quite highly priced.
You must run at night, ideally by moonlight.
Too bad my whole body aches
      and my movements are uncouth,
pulling on sweatpants, lacing up running shoes,
departing demands a protracted preparation.
and cowardice—I miss all of that so much.

*Translated from Russian by Sibelan Forrester*

Sibelan Forrester has translated fiction, poetry, and scholarly prose from Croatian, Russian, and Serbian, and poetry from Ukrainian, including work by Halyna Kruk and Marjana Savka in the anthology *Words for War* (2017). Her translation (from Russian) of Volodymyr Rafeyenko's novel *The Length of Days* is forthcoming from Harvard Ukrainian Research Institute. Her translations have won awards from the American Association of Teachers of Slavic and East European Languages and the Association for Women in Slavic Studies, and have been shortlisted for the *Big Other* Book Award and the Derek Walcott Prize. She teaches Russian language and literature at Swarthmore College.

# KOSTIANTYN
# MOSKALETS

A poet, novelist, essayist, translator, musician, and literary critic (b.1963, Chernihiv region), Moskalets is the laureate of numerous national awards, a cult figure in Ukrainian contemporary art, and a legendary writer–philosopher who prefers solitude.

Moskalets is the author of six poetry collections, prose collections, essays, criticism, and famous songs, including the most popular Ukrainian romantic ballad "She." He is the co-author of music albums including *Army of Light* (2008), which pre-defined the music of the Ukrainian resistance to Russia. His prose and poetry have been translated into many languages and published in international literary journals.

Moskalets is known for being a nonconformist. As an author, he is a representative of the generation of the late 70s and received recognition in the late 80s and in the 90s. Despite his asceticism and dislike of public events, he is a popular and important player in the literary space. Moskalets uses postmodern tools and graphically plays with words. His characters are full of irony and musical rhythm. In his work, Moskalets addresses the existential search of a person and the development of a spiritual personality. His prose is multidimensional, modernist, and noble; his poetry addresses universal themes, and his criticism is the voice of a meticulous intellectual.

Moskalts' family suffered from the repressions of the Soviet authorities, and his opposition to the Russian occupation in poetry and songs became the main symbols of Ukrainian activism.

Moskalts lives in Kyiv region, Ukraine.

## WAR IS NIGH

This summer marks 20 years since my father, the Ukrainian writer Viliy Moskalets, died. Perhaps that's why I've been returning to him so much lately, remembering his stories about World War II, his favorite words, sayings, jokes... All these years since his death, I really miss my father's presence, and now, the unreal and impossible opportunity to speak to him. To talk about what hurts. About family matters. About the epidemic. Or about the fabulous restoration of Kyrylo Rozumovsky's palace in Baturyn[15]. My father would most likely not recognize the palace now because during his life the palace was a ruin, without doors and windows, the basements alive with snakes, the upstairs teeming with bats, ready decorations for a gothic horror film, which (fortunately, or unfortunately) no one thought of filming there. There is a festive atmosphere at the palace now, cleanliness and order, the spacious halls are hung with paintings, displays fill the rooms, the wind gently sways the delicate curtains in the windows. The palace is surrounded by magnificent rose bushes and the friendly tour guides regale visitors with the history of the last, albeit token,

---

15 Kyrylo Rozumovsky was the last hetman of Ukraine, who died in 1803. Hetman is a political title of the top military commanders from Central and Eastern Europe. This title was assigned to leaders of the Ukrainian Cossacks starting in the 16th century.

hetman.

We could, after all, talk about the war. Not the war that is far away, but the one that is getting closer. The war that is nigh, undeniable, and irrevocable, no matter how much we would like to forget about it.

*If Ukraine joined NATO, Russia would not be able to swallow it. But this way, it's all useless.* My father spoke these words thirty years ago, right after Ukraine became independent. And I've remembered them my whole life as the prediction of a seasoned old soldier (my father served seven years in the army). As the summation of careful, long years of reconnaissance. As a warning, or perhaps as an order to us younger ones, those who will live in this, our country, defend it, and face the unfamiliar challenges of a new historical time. To respond with urgent necessity, quickly and resolutely, to threats from all sides, including those posed by our primordial enemy neighbors.

This war began in 2014. But I first saw and encountered it earlier. I saw it as a grand vision, sitting with half-closed eyes under the old pines at the edge of Emerald Field[16]. Shortly before I saw Milcho Manchevsky's film *Before the Rain* (1994), a beautifully shot drama about the war in Macedonia, a war between people who just yesterday were neighbors, Macedonians and Albanians. Going through the film scenes and storylines in my memory, sensing with my nostrils the approaching thunderstorm and the fresh scent of summer rain, I suddenly realized that this was

---

16 Emerald Field is what Kostiantyn Moskalets calls a large field near Matiivka, his native village in Chernihiv province. This glade is in the middle of a pine forest, it is sown mainly with rye, which has a distinct green color when in its young growth.

a prophetic film, that it not only tells what happened in former Yugoslavia, but also warns about what will happen to us, Ukrainians. Tanks flying the tricolor[17] unhurriedly drove onto Emerald Field, leaving black furrows in the young, green rye, confidently occupying tank trenches that were still there from Soviet times and had already managed to overgrow with barberry bushes. Combat helicopters flew from the northeast. The first explosions echoed over Baturyn, smoke billowed from fires which would destroy the capital of our hearts, just like three hundred years ago. Soldiers in uniforms without insignia blocked the Kyiv–Moscow highway, blocked the railway, and carried out the first executions of undesirables...

Under the sway of this terrible vision, I soon wrote several dozen songs, some of which later made up the *Army of Light* album that Viktor Morozov[18] recorded in 2008. Standing beside Morozov during the album launch at the Kyiv Artist's House, I thought probably no one in the crowded hall understood that this album is a warning, and not a product of memory or imagination. War is that which waits for us ahead, and not that, which is forever left behind. A few months after the launch, *The Ukrainian Journal*, a publication very close to my heart, kindly wrote the following:

"*Army of Light* could be considered a kind of reclamation of the patriotic song. Patriotic in the broadest sense, because neither Ukraine, nor any other country

---

17 Reference to the Russian flag.
18 Victor Morozov (born June 15, 1950) is one of Ukraine's most popular singer-songwriters.

is mentioned anywhere in these songs. Actually, this is unnecessary, as the main metaphor is already transparent enough. *Army of Light* is something much bigger than just the name of the title track. In almost every song a near fantasy level battle between Good and Evil, Light and Darkness takes place."[19]

Unfortunately, five years later it became quite apparent that my songs were about Ukraine and not in the least about some fantasy struggle.

Poems come to pass. Songs also. Eventually, many fans of my songwriting noticed the prophetic nature of "Army of Light" and other songs from that period, "Wolf Brides" in particular, as performed by the Lviv group Fayno. More than once, both in private and public, I've been asked the date that I wrote these lines: *"Darkness is taking our lands to the east, there will be war again for five years."* Those asking were mostly women, wives, mothers, and sisters of soldiers who went to fight in the east. They asked with undisguised hope that when the five years pass and this entire nightmare ends, their relatives and loved ones will return home safe and unharmed. Unfortunately, more than five years have passed since the writing of "Wolf Brides," and the war goes on; there is no end in sight, despite all my optimistic endings:

---

19  From Ukrainian Journal, №1/2009 (ukrzurnal.eu/ukr.archive. html/460/).

*Darkness is taking our lands to the east,*
*there will be war again for five years*
*for the first time my night without you begins*
*the bed like ice, wax rolling.*

*I love you so, that I can die*
*I bite my lips, but that's no help*
*My poor soul, you cut your hair*
*And hot tears choke my very air.*

*And so we've become the brides of wolves*
*Snow is falling, the veil is light*
*Crystals melt in the mouth and hot tongues*
*Lick the red blood of youths.*

*I love you so, that I can die*
*I bite my lips, but that's no help*
*My poor soul, you cut your hair*
*And hot tears choke my very air.*

*Spring will follow, with suns in the sky*
*The army of evil will die*
*Lands in the east bloom, the day*
*Of the gray wolves, free children, dawns.*

With tears in her eyes, a well-known poet recounts her visit to a hospital where our wounded servicemen are being treated. She was invited to come and read some of her poems to the soldiers, and so she went, carefree, like to any other creative evening, to her usual public of poetry lovers, far removed from military realities, smiling and tolerant of any verse length, theme, or lack of theme.

The ward was filled with young men without arms and legs. Without eyes. Men that no woman would be brave enough to marry. Their wounds were horrific; not all of them could be treated. Some of these fighters have already died, some will die. She read her poems to them, not knowing why she was reading them, but even more importantly, why had she written them at all? Who did she write them for, when in this world there are such mutilated boys, and with each day there are more and more of them? What important things could a girl, who with the exception of her beloved linguistic studies did not know the world at all, did not know that this world could so easily turn black and bloody? What did she know that those who had looked death in the eye more than once did not know? What could she teach them with her naïve poems?

It was they who taught me that evening, she says. They taught me to make do without words.

There are more and more of them on the streets of our cities. They teach us silently. With one pained look. With their appearance. Their message is simple, as simple as can be: the war is nigh. You must be ready. The time to be courageous has come.

*2021*

*Translated from Ukrainian by Irena Chalupa*

Irena Chalupa is a journalist living in Washington, D.C. She has worked for Radio Free Europe/Radio Liberty and the Atlantic Council and was a Fulbright scholar working in Kyiv, Dnipro, and Kharkiv, documenting dissident oral histories and training students in radio journalism. Since 2016, she has been an editor with the StopFake fact-checking NGO that debunks Russian disinformation and propaganda.

# SVITLANA
# POVALYAEVA

Ukrainian writer, poet, journalist, and public activist (b.1974). Born in a Russian-speaking family in Kyiv, Povalyaeva grew up as a rebellious Ukrainian writer and became one of the most notable representatives of the aught generation of Ukrainian literature. The author of seven prose books, a poetry collection, and a book for children, she began her work by writing youth subculture novels, developing the theme of freedom and protest against consumerist society. Her texts are modern and urban; critics have noted influence of the work of American beatniks and even ancient Japanese prose. After the Revolution of Dignity and following the war in Donbas, she found it impossible to write novels anymore. In 2018, she published her first poetry collection *Pislya Krymu* (*After Crimea*)—deep and poignant poems in which the themes of war, the passage of time, memory, and homeland are closely intertwined with the theme of love and sensuality.

Povalyaeva's essence as an artist is deeply connected with her activism. She took part in three Ukrainian revolutions: The Revolution on Granite (1990), The Orange Revolution (2004), and The Revolution of Dignity (or Euromaidan,

2014). Since the first days of the war, she has been actively involved in volunteer activities helping civilians. On June 8, 2022, her youngest son Roman Ratushnyi—a prominent activist who fought corruption and illegal construction in Kyiv and became a soldier of the 93rd brigade "Kholodny Yar"— died in battle at the age of 25 with the Russian invaders in the Eastern Kharkiv region. Svitlana Povalyaeva continues to support various cultural causes in his memory.

She lives in Kyiv, Ukraine.

\*\*\*

5 o'clock in the morning—
    in Kyiv, it's a kind of enchanted time:
The time of garbage trucks.
    The time of hardcore urban freaks.
The time of spirits, ghosts, and protectors of this land.
I stand on my balcony, as on the bow of a ship,
    and say to the fog:
"Glory to Ukraine!" A deaf response:
    "Glory to the heroes!"
So goes the "good morning" of village neighbors.
I twirl my cigarette. The smoke swirls with the fog.
Ah it's them! We usually don't see them,
But here they are—even without sleep—our defenders.
For the city dwellers, they are ghosts.
    Some of them actually are ghosts
from across the centuries, because how can you leave
how can you quit your land when…
when between 4 and 5 in the morning,
the missile strikes usually begin.

*2018*

\*\*\*

Even if you are a soldier and can't leave the war,
          you can at least walk.
An infantryman can learn the feel of different soils,
          of reliefs, and of distances
only the sea holds between its expanses of water and
          tectonic plates
in unreachable depths where there is no support,
          no oxygen, and pressure from all sides.
There's no support for hope or even for fear.
If you plan to cut down a tree, first shout "Timber!"
because in the forest you are not alone.
          On the ground you are never alone.
Lightning bolts multiply. A pilot increases the altitude.
A ship enters the Dnipro rapids from the sea.
Do you hear it, brother?
And over the internet there's only a green dot.
You're waiting: it will light up. And there we are.
You and I remain on that edge: between the solid, liquid,
the water, and the sky—and that is all.

*2018*

SVITLANA POVALYAEVA

\*\*\*

I just saw a stork flying above—a wedge returning home.
In the endless open sky, in which hateful rockets roam,
storks return to their rivers and nests, to small towns,
where the nested trees and rooftops of houses are burning
down.
On the streets lie the corpses of tortured Ukrainians.
Souls of warriors fly past the wedge of the stork to *Iriy*.[20]
And the stork flies home in a flurry.

*2022*

---

20 The ancient name of paradise in Slavic mythology—the blessed
place with eternal spring and the Tree of Life, at the top of which
birds and the souls of the dead supposedly live.

\*\*\*

Either darkness, damp frost, air raid sirens,
or silence—to hear how the brain boils,
how the body fears a siege.
A dog rests its velvet muzzle in my lap. His eyes shine.
I feel like the hem of my colorful sheer dress
that ruffles at the knees.
A May butterfly on a gentle wind over the highest hilltop
        in Kyiv.
Wounds are healing
in cement and stone.
You kiss me
cradling the back of my head.

*2022*

\*\*\*

This husband can be pierced by molten iron.
This wife can echo the pain.
This husband can embrace death.
This wife will hold her husband

until his last breath,
will think about death tomorrow,
or not at all—stunned as a statue.
She will sing at his pallored brow,
drain the yolk of a falcon's egg,
carefully embroider a linen shirt,
until he shudders with an inhale.

*2020*

## THE METRO BREEZE
## HYDROPARK METRO STATION

A sweet old lady is sitting and next to her a young man
      reads under his breath
an e-book about how the land was mined in Vietnam.
No, they aren't acquaintances or relatives—
      just metro passengers.
He is in camo. She wears a coat with a brown fur collar.
He's going to his military unit. She is going nowhere.
It is important for such ladies to move about—to ensure
      they leave some traces of their lives.
The young man runs his eyes over the lines for the tenth
      time—his thoughts torn by mines.
In this moment, the old lady asks what he's reading,
and he turns the screen to her. She shakes her head:
      *I forgot my glasses.*
He reads her the title, staring down the dark muzzle
of his black and red thoughts,
      and then, the table of contents.
Scanning to the first chapter, it turns out,
      is easier than crossing a blown bridge.
*It would be better, it occurs to him, if it were a book about diseases*
*that affect fruit trees or a romance novel.*
In his mind volunteer squadrons march to the tune
      of a popular war song.
The lady attentively listens to the text about mining—
like a concert or news on the radio.

She seems to be childless, but she has gone through all
        possible relationship stages with men
except for motherhood. Take off thirty years
        and she'd go through it again and again.
The young man started his weekend by donating blood
on an empty stomach, of course, then visiting a friend
in the hospital. The coffee machine on the way out
        declared: *Out of water.*
He stopped by McDonald's—a line.
        Long and rigid like a hipster beard.
Finally grabbing some shawarma outside the metro stop,
        a message came to his phone:
*Look, I think it's better if we don't see each other anymore.*
A response to his yesterday's:
        *I'm still inside you with my thoughts, baby.*


The young man in the metro reads aloud
        for the two-hundredth time:
*To lay out an underground stretch of explosives…*
The lady listens, looks out the window at the Dnipro river,
        swaying with the thrum…
*Caution. Doors. Hydropark Station.*

## POCHAINA METRO STATION

Let's hijack that rusty barge along with the old tugboat.
How many grains of sand did these vessels lift
        from the warm, yellow riverbed?
Let's sail upstream against the current
and on the barge's deck plant cilantro, strawberries,
currants, melons, wild and garden roses—
        the kind that billow unbounded.
We'll fly a Ukrainian flag from the stern.
You'll catch fish and steer our course.
I'll sunbathe and mind the anchor.
We'll sail at night, passing the flames of beacons.
During the day, we'll dock under the cliffs—
you'll collect firewood, and I'll wash
our stolen watermelons near the riverbank.
It's a slice of time I already long for—
        your movements, jokes, and habits.
Swifts and martins will laugh at me.
And at night we'll set sail,
building a fire between the cilantro and currants.
We'll lay down beneath the naked sky
        as stars shoot across it—never ending.

*2018*

*Translated from Ukrainian by Grace Mahoney*

Grace Mahoney is a scholar and translator of Ukrainian and Russian literature. She is a PhD candidate in the Department of Slavic Languages and Literatures at the University of Michigan and serves as the series editor of the Lost Horse Press Contemporary Ukrainian Poetry Series. From 2014–2015, she participated in the U.S. Fulbright Scholar Program in Ukraine as a Student Researcher. Her book of translations of Iryna Starovoyt's poetry, *A Field of Foundlings*, was published by Lost Horse Press in 2017. Her translations have also been featured in *AGNI*, *Alchemy*, *Apofenie*, *harlequin creature*, *Ukrainian Literature: A Journal of Translations*, and *Ploughshares*.

# ANDRIY BONDAR

Andriy Bondar is a poet, translator, and essayist (b.1974, Kamianets-Podilskyi, Ukraine). He studied history and literary theory at the National University of Kyiv-Mohyla Academy. Bondar published his first collection of poems, *Vesinnia ieres (Spring Heresy)* in 1998, followed by *Istyna i med (Truth and Honey*, 2001), *Prymityvni formy vlasnosti (Primitive Forms of Ownership*, 2004), and *Pisni Pisni (Lenten Songs*, 2014). The collections of short stories include *Morkvianyi lid (Carrot Ice*, 2012), *I tym, shcho v hrobakh (And for Those in the Graves*, 2016), the BBC Ukraine award-winning best Ukrainian essay collection *Cerebro* (2018), and *Lasoschi dlia Medora (Delicacy for Maidour*, 2021). He has also authored numerous stories, essays, and articles for various magazines. His poetry and prose works have been translated into dozen languages. He has translated over forty volumes of poetry, fiction, nonfiction, and scholarly works from Polish and English to Ukrainian.

His poetry is ironic and self-critical. His essays and short stories show how subtly he manages to feel the spirit of the times, and demonstrate the accuracy of his understanding and artistic reproduction of the world around him—the world of a person, who is not afraid to live.

Andriy Bondar lives in Kyiv, Ukraine.

## ETERNAL MEMORY

For some reason, I have never understood why we bury our dead so deeply. Sometimes, it seems there is something very symptomatic about it, something that is obviously indicative of us.

Although, on the other hand, it may just seem so deep, but it is a pit, just a pit. Some kind of special pit, which at the same time cancels many different actual meanings and transfers a person into the realm of pure memory. Also called "eternal." And there is always a scandal with this eternal memory. Nothing seems to exist forever. We all know that. Here, alongside, while we are breathing and standing in front of the square pit, where now they will put *not us* in the last robes and the last furniture, from which there is no way out, but only an entrance. Eternal entrance without exit. Eternal Ukraine with its eternal dead in its eternal black soil. The lid of the coffin, through which you look at eternity and through which eternity looks at you. And these people around, who find nothing more interesting in their lives than this vibration of tragedy, naked grief. People who dig forever in this black soil for eternal life in it. And at this moment, you understand how much you are theirs, no matter how much you run away, no matter how much you hide, no matter how much you pretend to break away from them. And you are standing in front of this pit, and you know that in fact you will be put there now. Part of you. Part of your kind—hard working, simple, conservative—first *kolyvo*[21]—three times—then *borscht*. And everything by spoon. Meat—by spoon. Try it, this is your day. Try with a spoon what you learned to do with a fork and knife. Spoon. Eternal memory. Then borscht. The red blood of our black soil. What we have learned to extract from it. Borscht, borscht, borscht. Red is not love,[22] it is borscht. And black is not sorrow, it is black soil. We know nothing. We exist. Contrary to. We did not want to. We got out, survived. We couldn't. We gnawed. We have only ourselves. We have something in common. We have always been here. We have one Eternal memory. "You can't say hello at a funeral."[23] I know, I'm not saying hello to you. I hug you. I kiss you. I love you. I'm not a stranger to you. Don't look like that. Well, eye glasses. Well, a beard. Well, the fingers that knock on the keys—knock, knock, knock. It's an empty sound for you, I know. Do you think it's easy? Well, yes, it's easy. It's easier than throwing manure, skinning rabbits, and dying. You die and live as if you know nothing else. And I live and I know that I have no one but you. And I know you will come the same way. Not you, then your children and grandchildren. Come and put me in our black soil too. I deserve it too, *right?* Well, tell me, *right?* My dear strangers. Strangers I don't have closer.

---

21  Kolyvo is a funeral dish of boiled cereals with sweet sauce. Kolyvo is a common dish that is eaten by the participants of the funeral dinner in turn.

22  Allusion to the famous Ukrainian song (Пісня про рушник) about the embroidered towel, which contains the words, "Red is love and black is sorrow."

23  A Ukrainian folk tradition.

All relatives. The whole family. You are standing. Crying. Black soil by spoon. Then borscht. What's first? Kolyvo? Or, maybe cooked peas?[24] Or maybe a sunny bunny?[25] There is no sun today. Today is a rainy day, wind and rain. And we have nine days[26] tomorrow. *Why nine?* It is only the fourth. Here everyone does it that way, so no wasting food after the funeral dinner. Everyone does that. Nine days on fourth. But forty days must be exactly that day because then the soul…tra-la-la. Or, maybe, tomorrow you will be taken away to the ATO?[27] Three children… *They will not take you.* They do not accept applications. *Kyiv returns our applications.* I have three children. I look like Shrek. I'm your cousin. I'm your third cousin—young, beautiful, with a button nose. "How are you?" Work—home.

We can't get to the cemetery with *our* person in the coffin, because there are two funerals ahead. We have to wait our turn. We are the last. We have to wait. Twenty-six have died this year. Four just the day before yesterday. One was buried yesterday. Today there are three. Six were born. 26:6 in favor of black soil. "Come to visit me, Ivan." *How can I come to you? I am alone now.* There were two of us,

---

24 One of the obligatory dishes at a funeral dinner in Ukraine.
25 The small dancing reflection of light from a mirror or reflective surface.
26 One of the Ukrainian Christian traditions of commemoration of the dead. On the 9th day, there is a commemoration of the deceased, atonement for their sins, as well as their blessing on the 40-day journey to Heaven.
27 The Anti-Terrorist Operation Zone (ATO)—is an official term to identify Ukrainian territory of the Donetsk and Luhansk regions under the control of Russian military forces and pro-Russian separatists.

someone always had to stay home—*koroli*,[28] pigs, chickens, ducks. Koroli—that's how we call rabbits, Andrusha.[29] She left, and I am now alone with them, with the koroli. She went into the black soil and left me with the black soil. And I will go to her someday. And I'm already thinking, even though I'm still crying, that I need a landlady. I don't even think. They think that I think. I'm a little over fifty. *Lord, why did you leave?* Why will everyone leave tomorrow, and I will stay alone? Kolyvo, borscht. I will come to you on Holy Sunday. Or I won't come. You see, the gate of the cemetery is closed with a lock. You can pass, crawl into the gap between the tree and the gate, but by way of the gate you can only be carried.[30] The gate has no wicket, no door. You can go through on Providna.[31] They will open on Providna. You will come. Or you won't come. And for now, crawl before you are covered.

Next time only feet first. Feet forward. It is wider in the head. The legs are narrower. We lie down. Still. And we move motionless. All of Knyazhyn is here[32]—nobody was buried here today. We came here because ours are also here. Ours are everywhere here. In Velyki Korovyntsi

---

28 Literally translates as "kings," but in Ukrainian villages, is commonly used to mean "rabbits."
29 Proper name: Andrew.
30 Reference to the fact that the gate is only opened to allow the funeral procession.
31 Sunday after Easter in Orthodox and Greek Catholic churches, during which relatives of the deceased come to the cemetery. The tradition of goodbyes appeared before Christianity and has pagan roots.
32 The whole village of Knyazhyn attended since no other funerals were taking place that day.

and Pylypy, Pyatka and Tyutyunnyky, Sudachivtka and Chudniv.[33] Today you can only crawl here. The great land of the immortals. By spoon. *Is this your first time at a wake? How did you forget?*

Lord, we have only you. And you have only us. Lord of sacred superstitions. Lord of the borscht. Lord of the black soil. Lord of the love that no one talks about here. Borscht is our love. Red and black. But mostly gray. In the summer it will be blue and yellow. But mostly gray. When she died, I had a heart attack, and half an hour later…they called and said…and half an hour ago I was washing dishes and had a heart attack. And my cell phone broke. And my mirror cracked. And now I will leave here, but I will leave as if I stayed here forever. It doesn't happen like that. Yes it does. They are not simple. They eat everything with a spoon. Try it, you will succeed. I succeeded today. My heart is calloused. The heart is the fluffy rabbit. The heart is an empty sound. The culture of cultivating Eternal Memory and nothing else. Everything else here is not culture. We're so used to it, Lord. Give us strength, Lord. Save us, Lord. Save us from metastases. We are the metastases ourselves. They kill us, exterminate us, burn us out, but we still live. Always not for ourselves. Always for someone. Bring a son to the people. Marry a daughter. Someone also lived for us—not for themselves. We continue. Chudniv, Velyki Korovyntsi, Rachky, Pylypy. Where will you run from this? Where did you run from this, never having lived here and even being born elsewhere? Why did "there and then"

---

33 Locations within the Zhytomyr Raion, northern Ukraine.

become your "here and now?" Or vice versa. Why can't you say hello when you really want to? Why can't you kiss and hug when you really want to? Love and grief…borscht and black soil…Ukrainian insurgent army. I will die you. I will live you. Wrinkled, golden-toothed, clumsy, wiry…

She told me, "When you come to Vysoka Pich, call me, I'll cook potatoes." I stopped by Vysoka Pich today and did not call her. I had time to mourn in a cold house. And her older sister Alla told me after everything, "Andrew, don't be afraid if Lena calls you. It will be me." That's what she said —"if." I'm not scared. I am ready. "I'd like five crimson carnations, please." "Five?" "No, of course not five—six."[34] Six born this year, twenty-six dead. Six years of serious illness. Everything is serious here. It was never different here. It will never be different here…because there will be no more of *us*. And only the wind, and only black soil, and only kolyvo. And only Eternal memory. By spoon. A big spoon.

*2016*

---

34 According to Eastern European traditions, an even number of flowers is brought to funerals.

# ANDRIY BONDAR

*Translated from Ukrainian by Liudmyla Glenn*

Liudmyla Glenn holds degrees in Ukrainian Language and Literature as well as Computer Sciences. For 15 years, she was a teacher and administrator at Dubno College of Culture and Arts in Ukraine. In 2019, Liudmyla moved to the United States where she began working as a medical interpreter. When the war began, Liudmyla and her husband moved back to Ukraine where they could assist family and friends and volunteer for humanitarian efforts.

# HALYNA KRUK

Ukrainian poet, fiction writer, translator, and professor of Ukrainian medieval literature (b. Lviv, 1974), Halyna Kruk is one of contemporary Ukrainian literature's most powerful and significant voices. She has published five volumes of poetry and two volumes of prose fiction. Her children's fiction has been translated into fifteen languages. She has won numerous Ukrainian and European awards for her writing, with her first recognition at the age of 22.

Kruk's poetry is characterized by intertextuality, apt metaphors, and unusual images, but at the same time, the language of her poetry is straightforward, informal, and full of the rhythm of living speech. Her poetry is about the meaning of human life. In her prose writing, Kruk explores and describes the experience of human maturation and growth. The importance of understanding the heritage of the past to be able to build the future is one of the central themes of her work. In her wartime poetry, the focus shifts to women's experiences of war. She often refers to God in her writing, and her latest poems sound like prayers—a mother's, wife's, sister's, and woman's in general—for her motherland and beloved people. Although Kruk herself claims that the poem must bring to light, her gut-wrenching poetry of wartime is a reaction to the ongoing tragic events, her way of speaking out with—"a spontaneous prayer, a terse testimony, a lament or a curse upon the enemy."

Halyna Kruk lives and works in Lviv, Ukraine.

## RUINS WITH A VIEW OF EUROPE

1.
to grow old from the news
to go grey from black smoke
to see through a hole flying
into a broken-down highrise
how the distant sun of Europe sets
I must rethink literary history
before laying it out to students
the ones who stay whole will need a different science,
the ones who survive will need a different world,
who will return our own to us?

2.
I don't put the blame on you, I'm only fastening
sticky tape on the glass in our great European windows,
in our bright European cities
            across and around the perimeter
the air alarm leaves no room
            for all the other kinds of alarm
don't forget to shut off the gas and light,
says the radio in the voice of my good acquaintance
and I understand that he's not kidding,
this alarm is in your air already, O Europe,
don't forget about the gas and light
accept us like bad news,
accept us like unpleasant medicines,
accept us like untimely childbirth,
that which is to be born will be yours
how sweet it isn't
how bitter it isn't

*2022*

\*\*\*

she went through and tried with all of you
though no one truly knew how it should be done

the good samaritan woman is a bad example

words come to her now just like that
like Jesus by the well, asking to drink

they marvel, they start jumping,
they show up as a different way of being

within the white walls of her house someone was cleaning
        a grenade
here are bloody blots, here are stains from drips,
a reminder of sin

share everything yours with me and I'll tell you the story
        of how
give me a drink—and I'll tell you how
to give it up

the good samaritan woman is a bad example

she comes to the well unaccompanied, thirsty
with a leaky vessel, with a bottomless vessel,
she scoops, she spills

words come to me just like that, with no occasion,
they say—we'll harm nothing of yours, give your whole
        self
they clean the grenade on my white clothing—bleeding,
nothing clean remains

where have you been, woman?
in this world, unsinging, treacherous, grubby,
you gave yourself to every impression, to every pain,
could not say "no," shut your mouth, stand up against

the good samaritan woman—a bad example

they come to me. ask me to turn away, so long as
they do evil, crush the grains of the grenade,
they're sowing blood

o woman, if you lack the strength to strike in return,
beat at the source
beat and beat

*2021*

\*\*\*

oh God, let the voice of anger not go quiet
the voice of those that sit in cellars, forgotten,
the voice of those that are left in the rubble,
the voice of those that cry out in brief dreams,
the voice of those that cannot shut their eyelids,
the voice of those that are wordless, mute and speechless,
the voice of those that shall die of hunger and thirst,
the voice of those that gather crumbs of courage,
the voice of those that stopped the columns with
      themselves,
that covered the defenseless with themselves from bullets
the voice of one woman that wails into nowhere,
      of one woman that calls,
that curses, that in grief buries her face
in a child's small body, in her son's photo,
      in her mama's things,
in rounded shoulders, in trembling elderly knees,
the voice of the house burned down, the voice of blood,
the voice of a mind that can't be sure what it is
the voice that breaks through the sirens,
that soothes the unborn and nameless
grant it a way out of the throat that's strangled by fear,
from a city under fire,
      from a body that will turn to ash and dust,
from a heart that beats from now on for every one,
      hear it, oh God,
the voice of hate in the world,
      where the voice of love can do so little

2022

\*\*\*

we'll come out from this changed, we'll come out. Howl
oh siren of the alarmvoice twixt Scylla and Charybdis
we're crumbs from the Lord's table,
            bones from an ancient crypt,
we're lily-images of underground temples,
            we're images of saints


you see us driven into alien lands,
            as if needles beneath our nails
at interrogations, that we're willing to give up for this
bitterest love, this land, these rivers, this branch,
this house fire, this ash, this carbon trace


from the one who's the cornerstone from God's slingshot
Out of rage at what is done to us, unable to accept
this, to see through whether to turn away our face
from the land where our most beautiful is left behind

*2022*

\*\*\*
the villas, sister, have emptied.
     On a spring ray as if on a spit,
we do not turn against people's glances, immodest, thirsty in the twentieth century with all that happened to us
     so much that no-
body among us was able to stay behind with our own
childish illusions, girlish reveries, pink dreams

the villas, sister, are looted one by one,
in vain our good mothers didn't teach us to survive a war,
occupation, deportation, death by famine, prison camps
they said instead to close our eyes if the bloodied road
leaves behind someone's body stretched out, torn apart,
     a body, yours or mine,
in the face of abuse, person, Lord, art thou here?

the villas, sister, are being renovated, it will all be
     forgotten, even if not at once, sometime
our sons will become full-grown,
     they'll trust in strength more than in us
our daughters, graceful as young deer,
     resistant as kevlar cloth,
stronger than steel,
     let them not be such as to touch wounds,
let them inflict wounds,
     let them be not even grateful to us,
their own unkind mothers

*2018*

***

while for this pain I have for you no nay
while for this pain I have for you no tears
and wherever we go now, he's behind us constantly
like a harrow under the skin, like a frozen scream, like one
of us...

I am Lot's wife, who looked back her last on the world

*2022*

\*\*\*

And Jesus came down to the Mount of Olives
in the town of Bucha, in the town of Irpin,
in the little village of Hostomel, in the village of
Motyzhyna,
and the little village of Borodyanka,
in the city of Chernihiv, in the city of Kharkiv,
in the long-suffering city of Mariupol
and begged the Father—
let this cup end with me

crucified on the cross worn on the body
of an unidentified mortal
in the year of our Lord 2022
in a soulless world

the sky and the earth pass by

*2022*

HALYNA KRUK

*Translated from Ukrainian by Sibelan Forrester*

Sibelan Forrester has translated fiction, poetry and scholarly prose from Croatian, Russian, and Serbian, and poetry from Ukrainian, including work by Halyna Kruk and Marjana Savka in the anthology *Words for War* (2017). Her translation (from Russian) of Volodymyr Rafeyenko's novel *The Length of Days* is forthcoming from Harvard Ukrainian Research Institute. Her translations have won awards from the American Association of Teachers of Slavic and East European Languages and the Association for Women in Slavic Studies, and have been shortlisted for the *Big Other* Book Award and the Derek Walcott Prize. She teaches Russian language and literature at Swarthmore College.

# TAMARA DUDA

## TAMARA HORIKHA ZERNYA

# TAMARA DUDA

A writer, volunteer, and university lecturer (b. Kyiv, 1976), Duda met early success with the publication of her first novel, *Daughter* (2019), which won several major Ukrainian literary awards. The novel has been translated into English by Daisy Gibbons for Mosaic Press (2022). A film adaptation of this novel is planned. In 2021, she published her second book, the detective novel *The Principle of Intervention*. She joined the volunteer movement after the start of the Russian–Ukrainian war and has state awards for her volunteer activities.

Duda's prose has pronounced autobiographical motifs. The action of both books takes place against the backdrop of the Russian–Ukrainian war; many characters are based on real prototypes. Her novels are exciting, emotional, and reliable reading, vividly and accurately describing the ups and downs of life during the Russian–Ukrainian war.

She lives and works in Kyiv.

## SECOND TRY

It was the second evacuation attempt—not counting the night she'd migrated from the bedroom to the hallway. The whole family had convinced her to leave the city a week earlier. Her daughters called from France, her ex tried... Actually, all her exes rang the phone off the hook—at least, the ones who were still alive. And she seemed to give in to our appeals. We ordered the tickets, got her things together, and enlisted the support of Zhenia Lebovskyi to meet her at the border. I have no idea when exactly things went wrong or why she ended up in her hallway instead of Warsaw.

We didn't talk for a while after that because I got stuck with the task of apologizing to Lebovskyi. At least her girls didn't blame me: they know their mother. And then things started up in Irpin, and they bombed the bridge, and I called her.

"Ira," I said. "Listen to me carefully. When you get buried under the rubble, young, healthy people will have to risk their lives to dig you out. They'll carry you out on a tarp, some bystander will snap it on their phone, and your bare legs will turn up in the frame. It'll get posted on the internet, and the whole world will be looking at your precious panties. You won't care anymore, but think about the poor soldiers: Why should they have to cope with this?"

"Okay, okay, dear. Why are you getting so worked up? I'm willing."

So I arrived at her place at nine in the morning, as we'd agreed. She'd promised to meet me at the door already dressed and ready, but instead, I found her in the middle of the kitchen in a nightgown and rollers in her hair. Can you please tell me who uses rollers in this day and age??

"Honey, I've lost my reticule," she said, rushing to me.

"Your what?!"

"My little bag, what do you call it now, my *crocs-body bag*. I have essential things in it, and I'm not leaving without them."

We spent the next half hour looking for her "reticule," each in the other's way. I emptied out drawers and cabinets, tossing piles of things right on the floor, crawled under the bed on my hands and knees, and shoved chairs aside. Meanwhile, Ira calmly dyed her hair in the bathroom and then came out with a little bag in her hands.

"Look, honey, I found it. Don't worry."

"You're kidding me. What do you have in that little cosmetics bag that made us late for the bus?"

Ira clicked the magnet. Inside was hair dye to cover the gray and two tiny rectangles of disposable gloves.

I didn't say anything, I just grabbed her suitcase, and we went to the car. Ira sat down, yanked the seatbelt, and then fiddled with the buckle for a while. Then she pulled down the visor mirror, took out a tissue, touched up her lipstick, and put the tissue back in her bag. Her bag slipped out onto the floor, she exclaimed, squirmed, reached down, and coins spilled out of her pocket. All of this was accompanied by a continuous stream of exclamations, apologies, and practically genuflecting—her mouth didn't stop moving for a single second.

I drove with my teeth clenched, repeating under my breath that everything in this world eventually comes to an end. My equanimity lasted as far as the first checkpoint, where it turned out that she'd forgotten her passport at home. Or maybe she lost it, ate it, pawned it, or accidentally put it in the freezer. "Oh my God, I don't know how this happened. I'm such a fool, I'm so sorry, honey!"

There was no way to turn around at the checkpoint, but if we'd gone straight, we'd have ended up driving along the river with no turns for the next eight kilometers. So, I had to reverse down the narrow lane and then turn the car around between the concrete barricades. The cars behind us were able to squeeze to the side enough to make a narrow passage. Ira leaned out the window, counting on her fingers, "This is how many are left; we're almost through!" I snarled for her to sit back because I couldn't see past her. "Oh, of course, of course, I didn't realize, I'm so so sorry, I'm creating so many problems…"

We got to the meeting point an hour and forty minutes late. I'd lost hope by the time we arrived; only sheer stubbornness kept me going. It was my habit of seeing every task through to the end, even if that task was shaking its curls and talking to herself, the radio, and other cars.

I couldn't believe it when I actually saw the bus standing next to the synagogue. It was a complete miracle, and I rubbed my eyes, not daring to believe the mirage.

People were waiting by the bus, mainly elderly Jews, since the Jewish community organization had arranged the bus. They stood silently: not touching, not chatting, no laughter or tears, none of the usual commotion that accompanies any Jewish gathering. It was like watching a movie with the sound off.

Each person approached the woman by the bus and got marked off on the list. For some reason, I wasn't even surprised when Ira's name wasn't on the list. The woman checked several times, then messaged the coordinator on Telegram and asked us to wait. Cell service was cutting in and out, and it seemed that the chances of Irina going anywhere today were diminishing with every passing minute.

While we were hanging out on the sidewalk, I noticed a woman standing entirely alone in the middle of the crowd. She was small, with gray hair, wearing a gray cloth coat. All she had were a bag over her shoulder and a battered easel at her feet. Her hands were crossed, resting on her shoulders, and she was swaying quietly in place.

You could almost physically feel the cloud of despair around her. No one dared cross the circle to approach her, to disturb this fragile heap of hopelessness. It felt like if anyone touched her, we could be flooded in a waterfall of all the tears in the world, find ourselves at the center of a nuclear explosion, or drown in a tsunami.

"We're each on our own," I thought. We can't save everyone, we can't even save ourselves. All I can do right now is hold back my own tears, push them deeper inside, and not think, never think about what I'm seeing. There will be time to process this later, sometime in the future, if there is a future. But now I focus on the present moment: Inhale. Exhale. Again. Now a rumbling is filling the air like a massive train. That's the sound of a Grad rocket. Now the earth is shaking. Now a ray of sun breaks through the clouds. Now a button has ripped off my sleeve.

Focus, drive away extraneous thoughts, be strong. Focus on survival. You will shoehorn Ira onto this bus, even if she has to ride on the driver's lap. You will not pay attention to someone else's thin legs in old-fashioned shoes next to someone else's easel. You will think about how they're going to comfortably ride in spacious seats and drive safely out of Kyiv, how they'll pass through the Zhytomyr region, and not one shell or bullet will hit them. About how they're going to have lunch, or better yet, dinner, near Vinnytsia and continue west without stopping. How someone will meet them at the border, take each one by the hand to somewhere warm and safe, and feed them and call a doctor. Surely someone will meet them.

"Where do you think I should sit?"

"What?"

She brushed her hand on my shoulder as if she were removing an invisible piece of dust. She looked like she could see straight through me.

"What do you think, should I sit near the door or in the back? I sat near the door on the way to Odesa once, and there was a draft the whole time. So probably in the back is better? But I'm worried it might be stuffy."

I didn't laugh, of course, just exhaled. And I think the people around us exhaled, too, and the circles of exhalation spread across the plaza. Shoulders relaxed a bit, suitcases were adjusted more comfortably, people approached the coordinator to ask about the seating plan.

The coordinator turned her head, looking for us in the crowd, and called us over.

"Ms. Rakhel—is that you?"

"That's me," nodded Ira.

"You're all set; go find a seat."

Ira-Rakhel turned to me.

"You know," she said. "It was easier last time. Even though we left Kyiv on foot, they were bombing us then, too. But I was five instead of eighty-five, and my back didn't ache."

I pressed her tight to my chest. Breathe in. Breathe out. I need time. Breathe. Breathe right now.

"Ira, you're in fine form today. You're not eighty-five. You're eighty-eight."

"Shh, don't tell anyone. A woman is only as old as she looks."

Granny gave me a peck on the cheek and climbed onto the bus, clutching her "reticule" in her little bird claws. I made it back to the car. Almost out of air.

Inhale.

*March, 2022*

TAMARA DUDA

*Translated from Ukrainian by Dominique Hoffman*

Dominique Hoffman holds a PhD in Slavic Languages
and Literatures from the University of North Carolina in
Chapel Hill. She has worked as a translator, researcher, and
teacher. Particular areas of interest include literature, art,
and cultural history. She is currently translating Ukrainian
fiction and non-fiction.

# LYUBA
# YAKIMCHUK

An award-winning young Ukrainian poet, as well as a screenwriter and journalist (b.1985), Yakimchuk is the author of several full-length poetry collections, including *Iak Moda* (*Like Fashion*, 2009) and *Abrykosy Donbasu* (*Apricots of Donbas*, 2015), and the film script for *"Slovo" House: Unfinished Novel* (2021), about Ukrainian artists persecuted by the totalitarian system against the backdrop of the Holodomor famine. Her writing has appeared in European and American magazines and has been translated into twenty languages. At the 2022 Grammy Awards, she performed her poem "Prayer" in English as part of John Legend's performance of his song "Free."

Yakimchuk has been personally affected by war: she lost her family home in the small town of Pervomaisk in Luhansk region, which borders Russia, and which Russian military forces occupied in 2014. Starting from her collection *Apricots of Donbas* to her latest work, her poetry embodies the story of a woman facing life's changing traumatic situation for her family, her hometown, and her country. Yakimchuk's poetry is versatile, often based on wordplay, combining both artistic subtlety and factual war-reporting style.

Critics point out that playfulness in the face of catastrophe is a distinctive feature of Yakimchuk's voice, evoking the legacy of the Ukrainian Futurists of the 1920s. Her poems are not just about the experience of war, but about identity reassembling, appealing to historical memory and attempts at its rebuilding.

She lives in Kyiv, Ukraine, where she has turned her attention to humanitarian work.

LYUBA YAKIMCHUK

## THE SMELL OF A SIREN

she ran a temperature at dawn
with the first ray of the sun
"weird," she remarked, and burst into cough,
"fever's always at night, but now it's in the morning"

she remembers for sure – on February 24th
she lay in her flat
and there was no one to stop by
to fetch her water, buy medicines
although she had planted lilac
and raised a son

oh well, Mykola, he's at the building site
and I'm here without mains
no way can I charge the phone or call anyone
or watch TV
just sitting here all alone like a spinster

she's not sure
the cough began
on February 29th or maybe on February 30th
she was spitting her lungs out
had no time to look up the calendar
"breathe in, breathe out," sure thing!

on February 39th she finally dared to look out the window
the street was empty and very silent

# THE SMELL OF A SIREN

"for real?" I inquire, nonplussed
I remember the 39th, it wasn't silent at all
"as real as real can be," she mocks, "silent like in a coffin,
are you gonna check my blood pressure or chatter?"

then water was gone
on February 53rd but she doesn't remember for sure
then a water truck came into the yard
she got in line from her window by proxy
and gave a shout to neighbour Yegor
to bring the bottles upstairs
"he had a crush on me in the 90s
I'd been a fox back then
so I decided to take advantage of him
although belated"

"do you have other symptoms?
can you smell? can you taste?" I ask
"smell only came back on the 71st"

she adds that she went out into the yard
for the first time in so many days
and finally smelled a siren

"no, you got me wrong
not a siren, I said "syringa," like "lilac"
and as for the taste, add to your notes
that all food is like cardboard to me
even now

*Vienna, May 10, 2022*

197

# CATS

from the palm trees that look like cats to me
(for everything reminds you of what you miss)
from the passers-by who don't look like my beloved
(no one can replace those you long for
whom you miss in the mirror and in your embrace)
I fly away home –

by plane across the Atlantic
then via Switzerland
I fly over the mountain tops
race through Austria and Czechia by train
and on through Poland
by a bus that is not on the schedule
then go by taxi
on I go by bike
that was borrowed to me just for a week
and see how I've delayed its return

I go on foot in my dirty sneakers
that I left at home
I walk in glitter shoes
that have never even been home
then I dash barefoot
on the tarmac and over the field
where two huge caterpillars
left slimy tracks

CATS

breath falters
cough worsens
heart leaps
but doesn't jump out
because I'm heading straight home
straight on

but I never ever get home
I never think
that cats don't look like palm trees
and that my husband
doesn't look like other people at all

*Las Vegas, April 4, 2022*
*Translated from Ukrainian by Svetlana Lavochkina*

LYUBA YAKIMCHUK

## THE NEW COASTLINE OF UKRAINE

the air, they said, so thick you could slice it
they didn't cut it – they riddled it with holes
thinned it out with missile launchers ("hail")
and rocket systems ("tornado")
trying to reach all the way to Kyiv

birds that flew in the sky
shat bombs
intermingled with people
down on our heads
following trajectories
now straight
now variable
only one commandment still stood
save your neighbor, destroy your occupier
only one commandment was actionable

an old man who couldn't stop vomiting
finally stole a tank from the battlefield
found the ignition button marked "mass," shifted gears
simple as that, let's go

women lithe and well-rounded
packed their suitcases with emergency kits and passports
tourniquets and bandages
packed their children and cats
packed up their lives, rolling them
so that more would fit in

a granny greeted the occupiers with seeds
take it, boys, let me fill your pockets
when you perish, sunflowers will sprout from within your
flesh
there will be beauty
trains glossy as serpents
sparkled along the steppe
half the country turned into refugees
half the country took them in
half the country stood up for them
half the country drove in aid and supplies
where did they come from, those two hundred per cent
of the general population?

the defense was still tactical
but the changes were tectonic
the Crimea broke off at the isthmus
shaking off the invaders
drifted and moored at Odesa
grew a triple chin of new shores

in the east of Ukraine
in the north of Ukraine
flowed a sea of blood
a Black Sea of blood
along the new coastline
and first medical aid
never came to the rescue

*Kyiv, February 26, 2022*
*Kyiv-Vinnytsia, March 19, 2022*

LYUBA YAKIMCHUK

*Translated from Ukrainian by Oksana Maksymchuk*

Svetlana Lavochkina is a Ukrainian-born novelist, poet, and translator. She has lived in Germany since 1999. Her work has been published worldwide. Her novella, *Dam Duchess*, was chosen as runner-up in the Paris Literary Prize. Her novel, *Zap*, was shortlisted for Tibor Jones Pageturner Prize, London. Both books in German translation were published by Voland & Quist to national critical acclaim. Lavochkina's verse novel, *Carbon*, was published in 2020 by Lost Horse Press, USA. In 2022, *Carbon* in Ukrainian self-translation was announced a prize-winner in Lviv's International Literary Competition, "Winged Lion." Since the onset of the war in February 2022, Lavochkina has been continuously raising awareness of Ukraine in germanophone mass media.

Oksana Maksymchuk is a bilingual Ukrainian-American poet, scholar, and literary translator. In Ukrainian, she is the author of award-winning poetry collections *Xenia* and *Lovy*, while her English-language poems appeared in *AGNI*, *Cincinnati Review*, *The Irish Times*, *Poetry Review*, and other journals. With Max Rosochinsky, she co-edited *Words for War: New Poems from Ukraine* and co-translated *Apricots of Donbas* by Lyuba Yakimchuk and *The Voices of Babyn Yar* by Marianna Kiyanovska. Oksana holds a PhD in philosophy from Northwestern University.

# OLEKSIY
# CHUPA

A poet, novelist, and translator, Chupa is one of the major writers of Eastern Ukraine, and a laureate of national and international awards (b. 1986, Donetsk region).

Philologist and chemist-technologist by education, Chupa worked as a machinist at a coke chemical plant, and at the same time wrote poems and prose in Ukrainian in a Russian-speaking region. He played punk and rock, and started poetic slam in Donbas.

Chupa's poems became a hallmark of the Ukrainian East. A bright representative of the Donetsk modern self-publishing movement, he is an author of three poetry collections and several novels. As a novelist, he broke into prose literature in 2014. His books, including *Bomzhi Donbasu* (2014), were included in the Ukrainian "long list" of the BBC Book of the Year award. His *Tales of My Bomb Shelter* (2014) was translated into German and performed by leading German actors on German Radio Theater.

Chupa is a multi-genre experimental author who documents and delicately elaborates on social traumas in his texts. His postmodern works are cinematic, voluminous, psychological, and deep. He often uses autobiographical motifs. His characters become guides to understanding the soul of Donbas.

At the beginning of the war in Eastern Ukraine in 2014, he lived for several months under occupation, and then was forced to leave his hometown. Currently, he resides in Podillia, Ukraine.

## THE GUYS FROM SHEVCHENKO STREET
(excerpt)

...If only the kids in Podilskyi talked a bit to their parents in the summer, they would have noticed the excitement mixed with anxiety that obsessed all the adults.

The speed of information spreading in small towns is almost at the speed of the Internet. No wonder that after a meeting in which the representatives of the town council voted unanimously to sell some land to Yuriy Ivanovych Shalapukha, by the end of the day all the adults were well informed.

The rumors started spreading. People were speculating wildly why such a well-off person would ever buy land in such a provincial town. In such a dump, in other words.

Someone was convinced that Shalapukha was going to build a *Pshonka-style*[35] palace. Someone was trying to convince everyone that Yuriy Ivanovych, following the most recent trend, bought the stadium to renovate it, purchase skilled football players for a renowned team, and win the Ukrainian Football Championship. There were

---

35 The opulent but tasteless style of the house of the former Ukrainian Prosecutor General Viktor Pshonka, a member of corrupt President Viktor Yanukovych's government, who has become synonymous with kitschy décor.

some others who believed that Yuriy was going to open a car service, taking into account the sea of cars flowing through the town and that there was no decent place to repair cars.

Some others hoped that a business-oriented local would start some sort of farm, maybe a poultry farm, just like during Soviet times: new work positions, agricultural renewal, and so on. Actually, this guess was the closest to Yuriy Ivanovych's intentions.

Shalapukha received the gossip that very first night. He laughed and even considered playing a trick on his compatriots. He didn't dare though, fearing that people might get cross with him. This wasn't what he wanted.

He simply didn't let the rumor spread and take weird and absurd forms. A week after the vote, the money was transferred to the town council's account, Nestor Sapka received his share, and all the poles in the town were decorated with notices that a new mall was about to be built and anyone interested might get a job there.

The town was buzzing like a hive. Jobs and decent salaries hadn't been a thing for a while there, and now Shalapukha was promising both. Kitchens, hairdressers, markets, and bus stations were filled with conversations about the new project and the one who initiated it.

...In a word, if only the kids in Podilskyi talked to their parents for at least a bit, they would have noticed the excitement and the anxiety. But no way, boys and girls spend no time at home during their summer holidays.

They leave in the morning and return when it gets dark. End of discussion.

Among the boys, who go to the local stadium to play football every day, only Zheka Shalapukha was listening to his parents' conversations. But he had his reasons.

The boy felt this growing sense of fear inside him. From the moment his father mentioned that he was going to demolish the stadium, the young one had no peace in his mind. He obsessed over it in his head and yet he couldn't picture it.

All his illusions and hopes were completely shattered when Nestor Sapka showed up at the stadium with a nicely dressed stranger. The boys were convinced that it was a recruiter from a football club, but Zeka was almost positive that the guy was the one under whose management the stadium was to be demolished and the mall built.

For the first time in his short life Zheka felt what inevitability was and, like most of the representatives of the human race, stood stiff, paralyzed, and waiting for the final punch. He felt like a tiny puppy, which is for some unknown reason being beaten, and wanted to run away from the town, from his house, escape, go where his feet would carry him, but he couldn't...

...another week went by, and a new week has begun. On Monday morning, all the parents went to work and the boys—of course to the stadium. Have you ever tried to keep boys at home during summer break?

Zheka Shalapukha flew toward the stadium, having a strange sensation. He did miss his friends. They would see each other every day but he never thought how important they were to him, what a big part of his life they constituted. All the teasing, calling names, shouts, offenses, and of course football, football, football! How much did he miss it all!

But as he walked out of an alley shrouded in trees and walked toward Shevchenka street, he saw what he had been fearing to see for a while. There were bulldozers parked in front of the stadium, workmen in filthy uniforms, and a few guys in white builder helmets who were moving around.

Moving his stiff legs, young Sharapukha crossed the road and approached them. Almost all the boys were there. They were standing with perplexed looks watching the guys who walked around the bulldozers, not paying any attention to the boys whatsoever.

"What's going on here?" said Zheka, pretending not to understand anything and passed the ball to one of the boys.

A few boys grabbed the leather sphere and disappeared behind the gate. Kicks were heard a few seconds after.

"They are saying some construction is going to start here," Hosha replied in confusion.

"What kind of construction?! It's our stadium!" ginger-haired Sashko got started.

"We've asked for someone in charge to come here and explain what's going on," Hosha continued, not paying attention to his friend.

"Hmm…," Zheka responded with a whistle-like sound.

"If they ruin our stadium, that's it, there will be nowhere to play football," Sashko shrugged.

Hosha gave him a sad look. It was the first time Zheka saw their leader so astonished and helpless.

"Boys!" one of the guys, as big as a bear, suddenly intruded, "Some rich man bought off the stadium. He told us to demolish everything up to the foundation. He's going to build something here. Some sort of commercial building."

"Fuck his building!" Sashko couldn't help it.

"Hey, little hero," one of the managers in a helmet, who heard the boy, didn't miss a chance to scold him, "Does your mum know that you, little shit, already know how to swear like a sailor?"

"I don't care," Sashko hit the mark.

"Wait till I come to you and kick you there, got it, little imbecile?"

The ginger-headed boy spit and turned away as if the message wasn't addressed to him.

"Hey, Vanya, start the engine!" the main guy shouted.

Bulldozer operators instantly turned the keys. The machines started. A horrible noise was heard as if numerous fighter aircraft were flying above the town.

The boys poured out of the stadium gate like water from a firehouse and gathered around Hosha. They looked at him with a question on their faces—what shall we do?

Hosha looked around and wanted to approach the main worker and try to talk to him again.

"Hey, mister!" he tried to shout over the roar of the machines.

But his voice was drowned out by the noise, and even the boys who stood next to him barely heard that "hey, mister."

The first of the bulldozers moved a few meters toward the entrance of the stadium. Hosha instinctively jumped forward, not sure whether he should run and stop the bulldozer or try to talk to the guy in a white helmet. Suddenly, Zheka Shalapukha broke out of the crowd of boys and ran wildly to the gates of the stadium.

He stood at the gate and stretched his arms out as if he was going to block a penalty goal.

He stood there determined as if behind his back was not an old and neglected stadium with a bumpy field but a fortress that he had sworn to defend.

The boys started shouting.

The first bulldozer, which was almost inside, stopped a meter from Zheka. The operator jumped out and together with the manager they grabbed the boy and tried to move him away.

"A-a-a-a," shouted Shalapukha in a voice as if someone was cutting him alive. "Why are you standing here, idiots? Help! They are going to destroy the stadium in no time."

The exclamation jolted the boys awake. As if following a certain signal, they bolted toward Zheka, grabbed him by his clothes, and tried to release him from the old guys' claws.

The rest of the workers hesitantly joined in, pushing the boys aside to make space for at least one bulldozer to get inside.

A messy group had formed by the gate of the stadium. Nobody could understand what was happening there, what was being said, and who was holding or pushing whom away. Everything got entangled as if in one massive bundle of yarn.

The adults and the children fought as one should fight to defend a fortress.

Suddenly a shrill cry was heard through all the deafening and unclear noise.

"A-a-a-a, bitch!" roared the manager, falling to the ground and holding on to his neck, "Ouch! This bastard bit me!"

He was still holding Shalapukha by his hand. The evidence was unquestioningly there: the manager's neck and shoulder were in blood and there was also blood on the boys' lips and teeth.

"Psycho, bitch!" shouted the manager, "Wait a moment, I'm going to show you who's the main one here, little bitches," he shouted in a scary voice as if hammering nails.

"Call the police! Call the ambulance for me!"

The guys around started searching for their phones.

The manager, too, picked up his phone and quickly called someone.

"Hello," Zheka immediately recognized a familiar voice on the loudspeaker. "What's up, Kirilych?"

"What's up, bitch?" thundered Kirilych, pressing the wound on his neck. Blood was flowing down. "We wanted to get started but there are some kids here."

"So what?"

"They aren't letting us inside, that's what. One freak almost bit down on my neck. Vampire, bitch."

"That's crazy," the voice became more serious.

"Are they there?"

"Yeah, all of them standing here. We already called the police and the ambulance. They are about to arrive. I'd say they should pack them inside and take them with—some to prison, the others to a lunatic asylum." He gave Zheka an unfriendly look.

"No-no," the voice of Yuri Ivanovych went quieter. "We don't want any scandals. We have to sort it out peacefully. Can you hear me, lads?" he addressed the boys.

"Yes, we can," Hosha took the leader role again.

"What's going on there? Do you want to go to prison or what? Now, leave and let people work!"

"Who's that jerk?"—Sashko couldn't help it again.

"Hey, I'm not a jerk. I'm Yuriy Ivanovych Shalapukha!" the voice boomed through the phone. "Now, leave my people alone. Don't make me come there and beat you with a heavy belt, you got it?"

Shalapukha hung up.

All went quiet.

Zheka buried his face in his palms and sat down. The boys were watching him. Some with wonder, some with disgust.

"Why are you all staring at him?" Kirilych even forgot about his wound.

"This Shalapukha's son," said one of the boys, pointing at Zheka.

He quickly got up and started walking away, wiping the tears on his face.

"Wait-wait," a few boys reached and surrounded him, not letting him leave.

"Where are you going?"

"Home," quietly responded young Shalapukha.

"Of course, now you're going home!" they started shouting angrily. "Your daddy is about to ruin our stadium, aren't you getting it?"

"What can I do?"

"What can YOU do?! The question, idiot, is—What are WE gonna do?" one of the boys, standing nearby, hit him hard in the stomach.

Young Shalapukha fell heavily to the ground, trying to catch some air with his mouth.

The rest of the boys led by Hosha pulled the aggressive ones apart from Zheka.

Kirilych, the workers, and bulldozer operators watched it all with some confusion.

"Did you know?" asked Hosha, moving closer and squatting next to Zheka and giving him a napkin from a pocket in his trousers to wipe off the saliva and blood.

"I did."

Hosha resolutely stood up, and approached the boy, who'd hit Shalapukha and punched him.

"If you hit someone for no reason again, we will bury you alive. He knew it and yet he still decided to be here against his father's will, not like…," he was about to finish his sentence…when something unexpected happened.

The sound of the ambulance was heard in the distance just as a police car appeared in front of the stadium. Bulldozer operators, using the boys' argument, quietly went to the cabins and were ready to go once they received a signal.

Once the police arrived, Kirilych ordered the

bulldozers to start again. The machines deafened everyone and started moving toward the gate of the stadium.

But red-haired Sashko, following a strange and unknown force, suddenly moved to the same place where young Shalapukha was standing just a few minutes ago.

He stood at the gate with his arms outstretched.

"Be gone, kid!" the bulldozer operator was shouting. "I'm not stopping."

The boy said nothing and simply watched how a scary massive earthmover was approaching him.

The driver—convinced that the youth will move aside at the final moment, that he'll freak out, give in, and jump away—pressed on the gas, and the vehicle jerked forward.

But the boy, despite everything, didn't move away.

A quiet crash sound was heard and then—a shrill and pitiful cry. The police, doctors, Kirilych, and all the boys ran to pull Sashko out.

The boy was unconscious.

*2016*

*Translated from Ukrainian by Olha Pushchak*

Olha Pushchak holds a Master's degree in History from Central European University. For the last 8 years, she has taught English in Asia and Ukraine, and she has been translating from English to Ukrainian since 2012. Some of her works, including short stories and fables, have been published by Svichado Publishers Ltd.

# IYA
# KIVA

Ukrainian award-winning poet, translator, journalist, and critic (b. Donetsk,1984), Kiva is the author of the books *Podal'she ot Raya* (*Further from Heaven*, 2018), *Persha Storinka Zimy* (*The First Page of Winter*, 2019), and *We Will Wake Up to Others: Conversations with Contemporary Belarusian Writers on the Past, Present and Future of Belarus* (2021). Her poems have been translated into English, French, Polish, Lithuanian, and Greek and have appeared in English translation in *Asymptote*, *Literary Hub*, *Los Angeles Review of Books*, and *Words Without Borders*.

Born in predominantly Russian-speaking Donetsk, of mixed Russian, Ukrainian, and Jewish ancestry, Kiva had to flee her native city for Kyiv following the outbreak of the war in the Eastern Donbas region in 2014. Her poetry has since described the incredible significance of home and her longing for it after losing it, the search for identity and historical memory, and the questions raised in turbulent times. Since the outbreak of the full-scale war in February 2022, she has shifted toward writing in Ukrainian. Kiva's wartime poems describe a young country struggling for its existence and freedom.

She lives in Lviv, Ukraine.

\*\*\*

is there hot war in the tap
is there cold war in the tap
how is it that there's absolutely no war
it was promised for after lunch
we saw the announcement with our own eyes
"war will arrive at fourteen hundred hours"
and it's already three hours without war
six hours without war
what if there's no war by the time night falls
we can't do laundry without war
can't make dinner
can't drink tea plain without war
and it's already eight days without war
we smell bad
our wives don't want to lie in bed with us

the children have forgotten to smile and complain
why did we always think we'd never run out of war
let's start, yes, let's start visiting neighbors to borrow war
on the other side of our green park
start fearing to spill war in the road
start considering life without war a temporary hardship
in these parts it's considered unnatural
if war doesn't course through the pipes
into every house
into every throat

*2016*

*Translated from Russian by Katherine E. Young*

\*\*\*
we've packed a contraband humanitarian aid kit
     of war songs
and shipped it to Europe America India and China
paving the silk road with great Ukrainian literature

what have you got there, brothers—
     they ask at the borders—
silence dressed up in cyrillic letters
the sacred fire of the candlelight letter "ї"
our and your freedom to rest in a land of love
like the broken trees of distant memory

what have you got there, brothers—ask our dead—
the history of a tribe with a dirty rag in its mouth
rotting chests filled with grandparents'
     and great-grandparents' lives
which we've carried for centuries
     as if shouldering the Carpathians

what have you got there, brothers—ask our living—
cloths embroidered with military chronicles
     and stretched-out sweaters of wrath
sloppy sketches mapping the new Europe
children's dust-jackets for future books

what have you got there, brothers—ask our mirrors—
copper coins of breath in our ripped pockets
the disquiet of air in the broken frames of our mouths
the pulsing streaks of time in our red eyes

*March, 16, 2022*

\*\*\*

How to explain my presence:
   the salt I'm holding turns to coal,
the earth becomes ash, and my body water.
    Why a tree needs a branch
is unclear, if you see the flowers and not the roots;
   but then
light mixes with fiction, and love merges with an island,
the path toward which it's never too late to begin;
   so that the river
pausing in winter's swollen embrace, forgets why
it left the streambed, the shores, the country,
   left the page; why
time, which is hollow like a clock,
    grows heavier before our eyes; why
an eyelid turns to stone; why translators work
in wartime; why war needs translators; why on this paper
there's a stain that can't be erased with a finger, only torn;
this mineshaft we're falling through is long,
    like hope's neck, but it too will cool
and silence's wedding rings are slipping from my fingers
like the shadows from our mortal faces, the old walls are
unclenching their fists and new people jangle
   in the building
like the coins from a broken piggy bank;
   why are we giving ourselves away,
like steam in the frost to mere nothingness;
   why are we stuffing
the chestnuts of words
   down unrealized generations' throats; why

are we walking, holding our breath, along the railroad
   track of history—they will tell it

again (and again and again) on our behalf;
        why are we looking into the windows
of a better world if tenderness for the poor isn't worth
        the music,
if there won't be enough money left to sing a single note;
        why are we moving
(not to a whisper) but toward that thread of water
        between a bird and the sky; why
do we call silence quiet fire, and carry stolen air
in the pockets of our shame; this tear-soiled handkerchief
        will never burn

*2021*

\*\*\*

you carry an unabridged explanatory dumpster
        in your mouth
this scratched-up bin full of paper weapons
which can no longer make a hole nor make whole—
death's iron water wells up beneath your eyelids

you flip through words, empty as white pupils,
that stink of war like an old disease
and you don't understand how the world
kept the bonfire of culture lit so long without burning
        down

you bring the list of the living to the post office of love
and you can't master the language of bitter silence—
time catches in your throat like history's broken clock
and gets covered by the dust of wasted lives

you walk like a stray dog with a cross in your teeth
you annoy the world with your excess presence
you pull the night by its long bell-like tongue
you lick the earth's body with your numb tongue

*April 3, 2022*

# REFUGEES

## [REFUGEES, THE STATION]

1

the long road home to a home no longer there
lays breath tracks through the station in Lviv—
people with death faces gaze at their emptied lives
the way last year's snowmen gaze at the war's first
        flowers

tears remain in their eyes like dried glue—
you can only tear off the past along with their eyes
to plant there the uprooted apple trees of time
grown on the dusty pathways of their palms

the rain greets the exiles with postcards from family
        albums
where war is always sitting in all the chairs
a bullet-hole in its mouth, smiling at the birdie of death,
as if at a joke that others just can't make any more

the world has studied the photo captions countless times
mariupol hostomel irpin borodianka chernihiv bucha
this cyrillic music hangs in the air like a long flame
drying under the fingernails with the foul water
        of shame

2

just one step, death, and we'll eat you for dinner
our old tin-can lives aren't your cup of tea
just one step, death, and you'll never leave this table
like a scratched-up tray covered in strands of free people's

hair
3


people step in puddles because there are no other paths
except to accept defeat like the free bread at train
        stations
into which volunteers slip the keys to future lives
if only we can find the strength to look love in the eyes


4


:war is the great defeat of culture:
they whisper these words on all the book covers
but the grass rust of war crimes has grown in their
        mouths—
and the amber-trapped silence gathers troops in its
        cheeks.


5


we hammer the evidence like nails into children's hands
        and feet
like nighttime talk that no one remembers later

look closer
the ash of this piece of paper
was once called Mitenka

*April 4, 2022*

## [REFUGEES, THE THEATER]

first night in a safe place—as we call western ukraine
you spend it on the theater floor like a prop
in this war you can watch for free
reflected in all the eyes of the terrorized creatures

[you can still buy a front-row ticket to world war three—
wrote a famous western journalist on the eve of the great
flood]

the lights dim so well
that the world can see the dirt under your nails
and your hair (grown out since your trip to poland)
that splits like branches on your jewish family tree
that a righteous piece of chalk marked with a cross

your nails are unpainted—eight years since your last
        manicure—
and when you read "for the woman from bucha"
(will schoolteachers discuss this photo in class?)
painted on someone's tidy cherry-orchard fingers
you ask the red nail polish: is the comparison
        embarrassing

but we, like the daffodils old women sell at bus stops,
are no longer embarrassed to be or not to be
like bitter bulbs that grow on the margins of history

this will be you in a couple of days, walking down
        freedom avenue (not a metaphor)
to leave all your prophetic dreams on the barbershop
        floor—
but this won't save you: for, like a madman
        with a razorblade of regret under his nails,

memory leads you across a dusty field of rotten tubers
and it's so long that you see soil where children's eyes
      should be

but for now you're lying on the theater floor like a prop
and you're shaking with the rumbling trams—
those civilian singers in the chorus of fighter-jets
and you can't pull the wax from the modern music lovers'
      ears

*April 12, 2022*

*Translated from Ukrainian by Amelia Glaser and Yuliya Ilchuk*

Katherine E. Young is the author of the poetry collections *Woman Drinking Absinthe* and *Day of the Border Guards* and the editor of *Written in Arlington*. She is the translator of *Look at Him* by Anna Starobinets and *Stone Dreams and Farewell, Aylis: A Non-traditional Novel in Three Works* by Akram Aylisli. Young's translations of contemporary Russophone poetry have won international awards; she was also named a 2017 National Endowment for the Arts Translation Fellow (USA). From 2016–2018, she served as the inaugural poet laureate for Arlington, Virginia, USA.

Amelia M. Glaser is a Professor of Literature at U.C. San Diego. She is the author of *Jews and Ukrainians in Russia's Literary Borderlands* (2012) and *Songs in Dark Times: Yiddish Poetry of Struggle from Scottsboro to Palestine* (2020). She is currently writing a book about contemporary Ukrainian poetry.

Yuliya Ilchuk is Assistant Professor of Slavic Languages and Literatures at Stanford University. She is the author of *Nikolai Gogol: Performing Hybrid Identity* (2021).

# OLAF
# CLEMENSEN

An icon painter, art critic, prose writer, and poet (b. Kyiv, 1976), Clemensen is an author of the prose book *Summer-ATO* (2015) and several cycles of poetry. After the start of the Russian–Ukrainian war, Clemensen actively joined the volunteer movement. Together with his wife, writer and artist Sonya Atlantova, he created the art project *Icons on the boxes from under the shells*, which has become one of the most discussed and original conceptual art projects in recent Ukrainian art. The proceeds from the sale of icons on boxes made it possible to maintain the work of the First Volunteer Mobile Hospital named after Mykola Pirogov during the eight years of war.

Clemensen's literary texts are very personal, tender, and metaphorical. He sees the world through a very peculiar prism. In the works, mythology, absurdity, childish spontaneity, and a deep understanding of Ukrainian classical literary tradition are organically intertwined.

He lives and works in Kyiv, Ukraine.

## SUMMER-ATO
(excerpts)

## HOWITZERS

Ten howitzers are beautiful slender fashion models. Take it to Paris for a fashion show—everyone will be surprised: how beautiful they are!

They stand and smile in the midst of a boundless field of sunflowers. Whether the field is decorated with howitzers, or the howitzers the field... I will take a photo of one of these beauties, and then, after the war, I will hang a photo of the beauty on the wall, and it will hang there for the rest of my life. And will ask her to sign it: *to Olaf with love, your howitzer.*

We have such howitzers! Even more beautiful than sunflowers.

And how they rumble! How they thunder!

There had been ten, and only one remained. And when we retreated along the border, leaving the encirclement, she followed us gloomily, sad, like a refugee, carrying a baby in her arms, picked up somewhere in the middle of the steppe, in the bushes. Someone left, and the howitzer picked it up. She bent down, wiped the snot, and fed it.

"Quiet, you!" nervously hisses at the soldiers, who began to discuss something loudly next to her. "You'll wake up the child."

The paratroopers fall silent. She has become strict now. She was left alone. And a strand of dirty hair came out from under the handkerchief. Her face is smoky, like a burnt steppe. Only the teeth are white and shiny between the lips, cracked from the heat when she smiles at the baby... Mother...

## FRAGILE GLASS

Sometimes the skin and bones of people who came under the fire of "Grad" become like glass.

The body is made of fragile glass.

Glass soldiers are taken out of battle carefully so as not to break.

Like a fish tank.

Doctors carefully do the surgeries on fish tanks.

Be careful not to spill the fish out of the glass container with the water. After all, one of these fish is the host of the body. You can't tell right away which one it is. And it happens that a lot of time passes until the fish becomes a person again, and the glass vessel becomes a body.

"Carry carefully! Look: what a crack there is. Add water, it flows out so quickly. Be careful not to let the fish swim into the morning fog."

## THE MOUSE OF THE KILLED TANK

The killed tank collapsed in the sagebrush. In sagebrush, they say, death does not smell like itself, but more like sagebrush and steppe. The chest of the tank is wide open like a door. On the threshold of the door, where the heart is, there is a small gray figure—a field mouse.

"Hello, guests," she greets us with satisfaction. "Go to the chest."

We are coming in.

The steppe bear, killed by the enemy, fell and rolled in the sagebrush, and the hunter took out the bear's heart from the chest, cut off the bear's paw, did not even remove the skin, and went hunting another.

"Now I am the heart of a hunted bear," the vole smiles at us. "Do you want tea? You know, the idea that the engine is the heart of a tank is completely wrong. The heart is in another place."

Then, after thinking a little, embarrassed: "To be honest, I don't know what kind of heart it is. When I came, the warrior was finishing it, roasting it on the fire. But for sure: the engine is not the heart. I am 100 percent sure of this."

After all, the heart is always in the chest.

Then I have been thinking about it for a long time (after drinking tea and getting out of the sagebrush thickets). What is the heart of a steppe bear? Is the mouse now the heart of the tank? And if she is a heart, then how does he live in the steppe with this heart now?

## THE SUN IS IN THE BELLY

An evening shard opened wide the belly. A soldier's entrails spilled out of his belly. The sky in the east was also broken by a heavenly shard, and there were clouds like guts in the sky.

He was lying with his head hidden in the twilight and was not aware of the similarity between the sky and his stomach. Ants crawled into the grass on his left hand, and the sun got tangled in his hair...

The sun hung in the clouds, engrossed in scrolling on Facebook (do not buy iPhones for planets, stars, and children). Because of this, the sun confused the sky and the belly (after all, they were identical), and sat down in the clouds of the belly. The night fell under the roar of artillery cannonade.

The war did not allow the sun to sleep. It turned from side to side, and the soldier suffered from this, daydreamed, and fell into darkness—even darker than the darkness of the Donetsk night. When he returned from there, the night seemed like a day to him, and if it were always like that, he would not need night vision devices, and the soldier would clearly see enemy scouts passing nearby with a mouse's cautious step. The soldier froze for a moment, and then the sun turned in his belly and he fell into darkness...

At dawn, the iPhone alarm went off and woke up the sun.

As if from a sleeping bag, it climbed out of the soldier's body, shook itself like a dog and, red with human blood and shame for its mistake, rolled up across the sky to the chirping of the morning bird. The cannons finally quieted down, exhausted, and probably fell asleep. So the soldier died in the morning silence...

## SCRATCHED AT THE DOOR AS A MOUSE...

Someone scratched at my door at night. Quietly. Like a little mouse. I opened it and was surprised—it was a tank: ours, wounded in the paw, standing in front of the door with tears in his eyes.

I went out to him.

"Poor thing! Do not be afraid! I will not hand you over to the enemy."

I took him outside the house, disguised as a stack, and began to treat him. And after healing, I quietly took him out of the village at night and released him.

"Be careful," I say. "Go. After the forest belt, turn left, and then go straight through gullies…that's how you'll get to our checkpoint."

In farewell, the tank licked my nose with his tongue: "Goodbye!"

After some time he returned with the infantry on board. And with a barrel of linden honey—as delicious as independence…

*2015*

OLAF CLEMENSEN

*Translated from Ukrainian by Kateryna Kazimirova*

Kateryna Kazimirova is a founder and editor of the Ukrainian art and literature journal *Craft Magazine* (craftmagazine.net). She holds Master's degrees in Philology and History of Art and a Postgraduate degree in Literary Theory.

# OLENA
# HERASYMYUK

# OLENA HERASYMYUK

Ukrainian poet and a paramedic with the Hospitallers military medical battalion (b. Kyiv, 1991). A literary critic by education, Herasymyuk is one of the most significant voices of the younger generation of Ukrainian poets. Her artistic and activist work distinguishes itself through a new awakening in the national consciousness. The fight for freedom, restoration of historical justice, and relationship between self and the outside world are the central topics in her literary work.

Herasymyuk was born in independent Ukraine, nevertheless, she knows perfectly well what the Soviet regime was from several personal accounts of repression as told by generations of family. Her project *Rozstrilny Kalendar* (*Execution Calendar*, 2017), the result of five years of documenting the stories of Ukrainians who perished in Soviet gulags, produced a great resonance. This underrepresented chapter of Ukrainian history alongside Herasymyuk's wartime experience as a paramedic formed the basis of her poetry book *Prison Song* (2019).

In June 2019, as a medic of the Hospitallers battalion, she took part in a special operation to capture Volodymyr Tsemakh, a man who was suspected of playing a central role in the Russia-backed militants' downing of Malaysian Airlines Flight MH17 on the territory of occupied Donbas. Olena Herasymyuk was awarded the Medal "For Saving Life" for personal courage, expressed in defense of state sovereignty, the territorial integrity of Ukraine, and selfless service to the Ukrainian people.

# OLENA HERASYMYUK

*Dedicated to Mykola Volkov, paramedic of the Hospitallers*
*battalion, who died on April 15, 2019,*
*while saving the lives of others.*


Our Father!
God of sovereign Ukraine.
I raise the phone in Thy Name.
I call Thy name into the handset,
I say: Bless you!
The boy Smurfyk and the girl Hera are calling.
Is this the One that art in Heaven?
I fear mixing up the call signs in the cosmos
and entering the Kingdom of Allah or of the Jews.


Our Father!
God of Sovereign Ukraine!
Our cell towers are fallen, I don't know if thou hast heard
my previous calls, but damn them.
Our Father!
Some bullshit is going on with the incoming calls.
The sky is falling, people are plummeting
take them to thee, they'll relay the message.


Our father!
Thy kingdom come. Thy will be done
if only they wouldn't shoot at us.
Give us some time, syringes, and tourniquets,
hemostatic bandages,
a decompression needle,
a bandage for a gouged eye,

diesel fuel, body bags,
armor for paramedics and drivers,
so that they bring all and well,
all our wounded, alive and well.

Our Father!
God of sovereign Ukraine!
The boy Smurfyk and the girl Hera are calling you.
We agree to anything Thou willest,
just give us the strength to survive it.
We agree to any kingdom of Thine,
so it won't be the kingdom of our dictators,
and from the other we will break through,
we are already tempered.
Let it be both on Heaven and on Earth,
but not like it was near *Ilovaisk*, when blood and earth
mixed together,
don't let it be like it was near *Vesela Hora*,
when souls could not crawl out from under the bodies
toward the Final Judgement.
If it weren't for Malysh, Valkyrie, and their shovel, they
would've been late to meet you.
Kolya, Pasha, and even Vitya, who
arrived in time for the first tedious lessons
at the old school in the village of Holoskovychi would've
been late.
So give Malysh, Valkyrie, and their shovels happiness,
grace, and health
forever and ever.

Our Father!
This is the boy Smurfyk and the girl Hera,
We will be old when it reaches you,
the war will end, another will begin,
we will die,
but as you can see, we will not lose hope.
Our time flies like a rope under load:
Grab it, half-burdened,
and if you want to stop it,
you'll smear your hands with blood.
I took our only line
a thin black thread between the world
and the trench,
I call my God from the floor.
While the Russians haven't killed us.
While no one has eavesdropped.

Our Father!
Do not give us our daily bread,
because it spoils without a freezer,
better give us cigarettes with a flavor pod,
a sensible mechanic and an order from
the General Staff,
because we are sitting here without orders.
Our Father!
Forgive us our debts!
We found cards here and played,
and there was no cash to give
because volunteers are church mice,
commissioned soldiers have credit cards,
therefore, nobody has lost, and nobody has won.

Only Sasha-our-soldier got thrown sixes on his epaulets
for the sake of laughter.
And do not forgive our enemies –
they killed first.
How can we forgive, Lord, how can we forgive?
Each shell, each bullet, is signed by them
in our names:
"Here's for you, *ukrop*,[36] from the people of the Donbass."
What fucking Donbas are you from? Vladikavkaz?
Ours haven't been there since the days of the Gulag!

Our Father!
Seest Thou what a clusterfuck we have here?
Our Father, give us orders and live ammo
Let Thy will be done in our land.
Forgive us for losing our final accounts,
and on sad days,
and on dark days,
the Unclean we can handle ourselves
and don't tempt me to kill myself neither in civilian life,
nor on the front line,
because some of us came just for this.

Our Father!
The boy Smurfyk and the girl Hera are calling you.
Relay our greetings to the Holy Spirit, the Father, and the
Son

---

36 Literally means "dill" from Russian. Ethnic insult which Russians
used to call Ukrainians with the beginning of the war in 2014. Based
on the consonance of the first three letters in the words "Ukrainian"
and "ukrop."

Forever and ever. Copy that.
Over.
Father on High!
Cell towers are falling on us.
Father on High!
I know there's almost nothing for us
Take me, whenever you want,
So I may speak to you live.

*2019*

*Translated from Ukrainian by Charles Bonds*

Charles Bonds holds a doctorate in history from Indiana University. He is the Vice-President of Art and Soul of Ukraine, an organization that supports artists, art therapy, and beautification projects in Ukraine. He teaches English in Lviv, writes poetry and prose, volunteers, and paints digitally and on canvas.

# YULIYA
# MUSAKOVSKA

Yuliya Musakovska is a Ukrainian poet and translator, a member of PEN Ukraine (b. 1982, Lviv). She is the author of five poetry collections, *The God of Freedom* (2021), *Men, Women and Children* (2015), *Hunting the Silence* (2014), *Masks* (2011), and *Exhaling, Inhaling* (2010). A translator of Tomas Transtromer into Ukrainian and of Ukrainian authors into English, her own poems have been translated into English, German, Spanish, Hebrew, Lithuanian, Estonian, Norwegian, Polish, Bulgarian, Chinese, and other languages. Yuliya is the recipient of numerous literary awards in Ukraine, including Krok Publishing House's DICTUM Prize (2014), the Smoloskyp Poetry Award (2010), the Ostroh Academy Vytoky Award (2010), the Bohdan Antonych Prize (2009), and the Hranoslov Award (2008).

The poetry of Musakovska's early collections is deep, feminine, and somewhat melancholy; it shows the author's hypersensitive understanding of the world and develops the theme of relationship between man and woman. The collection *Men, Women and Children*

(2015) grasps the most important themes of that time: changes, losses, and war, but leaving a place for hope. Her *The God of Freedom* and most recent poems are clear, concise, and, at the same time, voluminous. Her work provides a certain summary, a snapshot of personal and historical events, an exploration of the limits of love, and exploration of the country.

She lives in Lviv, Ukraine.

YULIYA MUSAKOVSKA

## MY MOTHER'S PRAYER

I hear my mother crying for the very first time,
over the phone.
A steady bright flower, my mother.
A beauty from the Caucasus, at sixty-eight.
A safe harbor and its citadel.
Mother of mine, a human embodiment of
the Ten Commandments,
support and consolation for her neighbor.

*How can humans do this to other humans?*
*How is it possible?*
*Why hasn't the earth swallowed them,*
*these brutes,*
*why hasn't it pushed them back into its womb?*
*Why hasn't lightning struck them?*

The barbarian stinks of alcohol fumes and rot,
tearing up the new day's throat
with dirty ravenous fingers.
He breaks bones, reveling in killing
of everything living
in the ecstatic ritual of self-destruction.

Mother, my flower, don't cry.
You will finally see how darkness consumes them,
how Christ is temporarily being replaced
by the severe God of the Old Testament.

*March 2022*

*Translated from Ukrainian by Olena Jennings and the author*

## THE DOVE

While you are catching a dove,
your father laughs behind his glasses,
like the boy he will always be.
The wind from the lake becomes stronger, he lifts
        his hood,
and he resembles a polar explorer,
a penguin-turner (Hannusia, nothing is forgotten).
You pull a hat over your ears, quickly,
        without being reminded.
I wonder, what it is like to be under constant quiet care,
when someone holds an invisible umbrella above you
in bad weather,
when the heavens blare like car horns at rush hour.
A presence, which you can feel at any distance,
a familiar voice in your head: don't be afraid, go toward
        the light.
The thick soles of your shoes,
the threads between you thin and strong,
a radio signal impossible to silence or turn off.
His face remains in a frame, tanned, weathered.
Pebbles, shells, coins in pockets,
salt on a child's lips.
When you grow up, you'll become a movie star
        or a doctor.
While you are catching the dove,
        I am catching your father.

*2015*

# THE NEXT SON

and the name that she calls her next son is anger
in his backpack, she puts fragments of peace
from the door in the neighbor's apartment, dense
blinding flashes of light or voices of fire burst

fists full of keys and at the exit darkness and smoke
his hand will tremble, the keys clanging like brass bells
dragon's teeth have already been sown so warriors
        will emerge
and the walls will shake and quietly follow him

what he took on this road is crumbled somewhere
        on the bottom
white doves from breadcrumbs the word the body
squeezed together in a child's palm are flowers and arrows
with sharpened ends and icy petals

now it's not funny not frightening that the fire ate
        through iron
it tore off all the hinges and opened the doors wide
here is the point of no-return and on the frozen water
the feet of her next sons will clatter

*2014*

## HOW WILL WE RETURN?

how will we ever return, my sister
digging the prickly hawthorn from beneath our nails
shadows have worn out sungods have aged
our hearts radiate fear and hunger
how is it possible to hear the rustling of the grass
when its roots have been charred beneath your feet
the eyes of abandoned buildings dark blown out
letters from books thickly scattered like bullets
letters scorched blackened – bones crackle –
who will be able to put them together to form words
time to return sister don't let go of my hand
we will run barefoot over the broken glass incredibly fast
believing in the lindens shedding leaves in these
                cold rivers
believing even if obstructed, never giving up

look at the way silver haired ladies wash banners
                in the river
carefully cherishing they bathe them like infants

*2015*

## THE SURVIVORS

We will make a dugout, get ourselves a goat,
we will have a piece of the yard, like a Viennese park.
At night the tooth of the moon shines in its mouth,
turning each of us into a burnt crisp by morning.
A handful of warm ashes, a handful of dried strawberries.
Our small joys, our large grief.
Laughing, you seem careless and mean.
You squeeze the handle of the shovel as if it is an enemy's
         throat,
I choke because it feels like it is mine.
Look, forget-me-nots have blossomed on forearms.
The spring thunder – Gabriel amuses himself this way
with our names in the vocative case.
Children of the charred garden, the burnt roads.
How can it be now – to plant it in the earth so that it
         sprouts?
To drink milk with a bloody aftertaste
while the shadow of a manhunter circles above.
Making nests on pear trees – should we cut them all
         down?
Stand to face me, quiet, like grass.
The night passes. We step over cold dew.
We will thrive. We will survive.

*2015*

YULIYA MUSAKOVSKA

*Translated from Ukrainian by Olena Jennings*

Olena Jennings is the author of the poetry collections *The Age of Secrets* (Lost Horse Press) and *Songs from an Apartment*. Her novel *Temporary Shelter* was released in 2021 from Cervena Barva Press. Her translation of Vasyl Makhno's poetry collection, *Paper Bridge*, was published by Plamen Press and her translation with Oksana Lutsyshyna of Kateryna Kalytko's collection *Nobody Knows Us Here and We Don't Know Anyone* is forthcoming from Lost Horse Press. She is the founder and curator of the Poets of Queens reading series and press.

# OLENA
# STIAZHKINA

OLENA STIAZHKINA

A prose writer, historian, and publicist (b. 1968, Donetsk), Stiazhkina lived and worked in Donetsk until 2014 and has previously written mostly in Russian. She is a winner of several prestigious literary awards for Russian-speaking writers. Stiazhkina is the author of many novels and short stories, along with important historical monographs. After the start of the Russian–Ukrainian war, she was forced to move to Kyiv. She is also known as the Founder of the civil movement De-occupation. Return. Education. The moment of transition in her work to writing in the Ukrainian language is depicted in the bilingual novel *Cecil the Lion's Death Made Sense* (2021). She is also an author of *Zero Point Ukraine: Four Essays on World War II* (2021), where Stiazhkina offers a new understanding of what happened in Ukraine before, during, and after World War II.

Stiazhkina's prose, whose roots can be found in detective literature, is organized and meticulous. Stiazhkina relies on the psychological development of her characters and the beauty of a refined language.

She lives and works in Kyiv.

## AFTER THE GRAPE, PERHAPS
(excerpt)

They call her Lidia. After the grape, perhaps. And him, Mykola. They both do not permit anyone to shorten or disfigure their names with nicknames. When they go for walks, Lidia likes to look at the birds, but she does not always know what they are called. Lidia takes photographs and then googles them. Some birds turn out to be blue tits; others, magpies. The swans watch Lidia. They are very big. They are always very big.

"They're like dogs, aren't they, Mykola?"

"Nothing of the sort," he says. "Not at all."

When they go for walks, Mykola likes to look at the people drinking coffee. Lattes, cappuccinos, espressos. Large and small paper cups. Plastic lids... He also likes to look at the people drinking tea. But there are not as many of those. For every three cups of coffee, there's one of tea.

"Why is that do you think?" he asks.

"I don't know," says Lidia.

"Shame." He gets angry, because Lidia. Full stop. Because Lidia, and that's it.

Mykola gets annoyed because the time for love still has not come along, but Lidia came along and now there is nothing else he can do. Or indeed to the contrary: now everything had to be changed and cancelled. Mykola would like to have some space so that he could potentially, or potentially not, study some more, see the world, count the lattes and cappuccinos say, in Bern or Amsterdam, compare the number of cups left beside stations, hospitals, libraries, and parks, so that he could sleep without undressing, without shaving, if he felt like it... But then Lidia took his hand and asked, "What's the wifi password here?"

His answer: "Hey, stop pawing me."

The "hey" had the right effect, not offensive, but the tone was clear enough.

He said: "It's not for everyone. Each person has their own."

"So, it looks like I'm without internet," she sighed. "So, now I have to make conversation?"

Lidia knows what he wants to say: *Please, only not with me.* It was written on his face. She was able to read his face; she had learned almost right away. Fortunately, not totally and not with full accuracy. Mykola convinces himself that it is impossible to guess his thoughts completely: if so, it would frighten her off. Because his next thought was about the pose that he, that they, could do it in. The sex was not as mechanical as building something from Lego, but it was missing some details. What was missing was... Well, he needed to think more about this, but he could not. It was easier to think about starting a new way of life full of studying, not shaving, sleeping without undressing, and seeing the world. Seeing the world: each of his pointed *Oh yeah?!*s was a cry out for this.

"Can I ask a forward question?" Lidia whispered to him.

He did not have time to answer before she fluttered by his all-too-lonely ear: "Are you wearing any underwear?"

"Nothing. No wifi, no conversations, and no underwear," he whispered to her.

Lidia herself did not know why she kissed him. She says his ear was nearby, that it smelled nice and that it was like a sparrow. And she had always wanted to kiss a sparrow. Especially its stomach. Its tummy. She says this sitting at the dinner table, she says this to his parents at Christmas dinner, what is more. Mykola's father tries as hard as he could to retain a semblance of composure, to act like a mature and wise person, but obviously he cannot stand it any longer and starts shrieking. Mykola and all his friends recognize this unrestrained, obscene laughter that comes out through his face, his body, his gaping eyes and even his snorting...

"My life will now never be like it was before, Lidia," says his father. "Never."

And his mother... His mother also snorts, most likely thinking about what his father's ear looks like. His mother strokes his father's head, who then says: "Don't you dare! Stop that!"

"You think it wouldn't be possible?" asks Lidia, and sighs softly. "All right. I'll just eat all your delicious food then."

Lidia is not embarrassed. She loves it when people laugh and she loves to eat, but she is still a little shy. Mykola's mother once asked her: "What should I make you? Do you eat meat?"

Lidia shook her head: *No.* But then she tried to shake it back again, because her "no" didn't concern meat as an object of appropriation, but meat as a temporal placeholder. Lidia is studying anthropology. But even anthropologists cannot shake their heads back again. Therefore, she had to shake back with the words: "It's not like I never eat it. Just not often."

When Lidia eats, she doesn't cease to be amazed. According to Paul's letter to the Corinthians, if something is constant and never changes, then this is love. Although... Although Lidia is not sure whether she understood everything at the seminary properly. Lidia never ceases to be amazed by pesto, by the sound of swans flapping their wings, by her own name, by how Mykola can play chess, football, and poker.

Mykola wants to buy a mobile coffeehouse. Not one that needs to be towed to its spot, but one that can drive by itself. A coffeehouse on wheels that he could even live in, in case of anything. That is, if the winter is not too harsh, and parking is permitted. He could go to Bern, for instance, to the mobile coffeehouse convention.

"Or they could just come here. Let's hold the conference ourselves, and they could just come here, if they're not too scared," says Lidia. "And I can research them. I will finally find out whether latte people differentiate from cappuccino people."

"And what's your working hypothesis?" asks Mykola's father.

"Latte people can live alone, whereas cappuccino people cannot. The question isn't to do with the quality of the coffee, but with the number of sips before they taste the bitterness. Latte people reach this point later. People who aren't bitter can live alone."

"Debatable. It's more likely to be the other way around," says Mykola.

He does not just say things; he also does them. Mykola ran away from Lidia three times. "Run away" is a figure of speech. Mykola disappeared three times. He didn't call, answer his messaging app, or go online. *From now on,* Lidia wrote to him, *we can never explain to our children what a messenger app is. Do you understand me? For them, it'll have to be a pager or a landline telephone. Then no-one will believe that you acted so idiotically. When I imagine someone with a pager, they seem so dusty and ancient, like a pithecanthropus. They will think you're just the same.*

Mykola wants to ask, *so what is a pithecanthropus,* but google exists for looking up curiosities of this kind.

Only bitter people can live alone. For everyone else, solitude is like rain: it's not a tragedy, but one would do better to have a plastic mac or umbrella for protection. In essence, Mykola is an espresso person. If people like milk, then let them drink milk. *Lidia, stop pawing me.*

In truth, each of those three times, he did not want Lidia to stop pawing him. Under different circumstances, he would have been the one to choose her. He would have chosen only her, to be precise. Because she is funny, because she has dark hair and dark eyes and small hands and a mouth that lives its own full and busy life. But even if her hair was blonde, and her eyes were blue, if her hands were like garden rakes, and her mouth was as thin as a shoelace... If she was but a terrible shadow, he would have chosen only her.

The third time was the longest. Lidia finally got offended and only wrote to him once a day. She deliberately chose the most revolting and most indifferent letters she could when she wrote to him. She chose consonants like the concussed *k* and *t*, and vowels like the whiny *i* and arrogant *a*. Plus an ugly and suspicious question mark.

Mykola was writing his Master's thesis and tried to regain his football skills. Writing was more painful than playing football because someone who wants to sell coffee cannot understand why they would need to know hydrogeological conditions and the characteristics of the quality of potable groundwater at the Znamianske deposit in Kirovohrad oblast. Why all of this? Why is Mykola now a geological engineer? Was there no place he could stuff away this diploma and forget about it forever?

"Potable groundwater—that's an interesting point, you know," Lidia would have said to him. "Not every guy can make hot drinks with groundwater, but you can." But she didn't get to tell him so.

Lidia does not remember all of this. Lidia always has a bunch of ways to forget bad and stupid things. Lidia during that time went on an expedition to speak to buildings which have birds living in them. Some birds live as birds should, sleeping on rafters and flying in under the eaves to warm themselves. Other birds are like the English royal family and settle into the heart of the building alongside the people. When these birds are not taken out onto the balcony and only circle about in a cage, their inner life has almost no correspondence with their outer contours. Parrots and canaries live inside the houses. Outside live pigeons, sparrows (in bulk), and sometimes crows and titmice.

"We ate the bullfinches," Lidia says and laughs. Her

task was to understand why birds choose some buildings and not others and whether they always did so. Whether man, building, and bird have always lived together and whether they always knew that they lived together.

"Let her be," said Mykola's father. "You're in the wrong here. Why are you hiding yourself away from her like this? You know, well… That's my point."

"Did mum tell you to say that?"

"I know how it is."

They all knew how it is. All three of them. Mykola's mother and Lidia's mother and Mykola's father. They all know how it is, but in very different ways. Lidia says that when children go to school, parents lose their first names. Mykola disagrees. His parents lost their first names much later and, it seems, they still had not had time to get used to it.

When Mykola's mother was still Kateryna, or Katya, when she flew from town to town, from country to country, to become the best salesperson of household chemicals and home cosmetics there was, when she stopped for a minute in the kitchen to see how Mykola had grown or how his voice had changed, she always asked what he was reading and whether he was sexually active. Mykola got offended, because he did not read books and, well, whose business is it anyway, and he blushed, because… Because whose business it is anyway. Mama Katya laid her hands on her breasts and gave a speech about the benefits of condoms, finishing it on a high note: "If the girl gets pregnant, you must marry her!"

"That's a very strange way of getting married," Mykola huffed.

"But girls do that, you see."

"I'll make sure to remember."

Mykola's father was Oleh. He did not speak about the benefits of condoms, he only talked about lorries, rest stops, diesel fuel, prepayment, roads, and work partners, some of whom were his friends.

But now they both talked about Lidia and about him. His mother had stopped asking him whether he was sexually active.

"I love you, and I will keep loving you," Mykola wrote after three weeks of Lidia's inane *how-are-you*ing. He did not send it. Then he wrote it again and did not send it. And again, and again. And then he went to Lviv, where, according to her hypothesis, birds and people have been living together for a long time. Which is why Lviv was the right place to tell Lidia that she was stupid, pecking away at things like a woodpecker, and it was time to change the record. It was time to learn how to write something different to the stubborn and soulless *How are you?*

Lidia took photographs of the buildings and recorded birdcalls on her phone. Lidia did not run up to him, so that he would not have to run. He went as was most comfortable for him.

And yes, he was not wearing underwear. There he was, in the ward, with no wifi and conversations, and no underwear. He was missing half his leg for sex, although he still had his knee. Now Mykola understands that he is very lucky to retain his joint. Yet he still closes his eyes in order not to see himself in the mirror. Mykola starts the day with the words, *Massachusetts, come to me!* Massachusetts is a nickname. The name for his prosthesis. When the time comes to replace it with a new one, it will be a shame to part with it. Lidia offers to leave Massachusetts some food at night: Lidia thinks that Massachusetts likes to eat seeds. For Lidia, everything good and useful in the world is to do with birds.

But for Mykola everything is like a bad dream. A nightmare. He screams and wakes up in a sweat if he dreams of the war, or if in his dream Lidia goes up to someone else's bed on that first day in the ward. He tends to dream more about the war than anything else. For now, he cannot talk about it. He wants to be strong, beautiful, and whole. But if he had to do it all again, he would have made all the same choices. Including Lidia.

"Enough of your hypotheses," says Mykola's mum. "They always seem to know how it is better than we do… Enough."

"That's my point," answers Mykola's father. "That's just my point."

"Muuuum!" Mykola whined. "Can you not just… Just give me the 'no-tears' shampoo, ok?"

Lidia leans over to the bowl of apples, takes one, looks at it, raises it to her mouth, which continues to live its full, slightly marred, but very intense life, but then she stops and fails to take a bite. She turns her head to Mykola and asks, "Would you like one?"

*February, 2019*

*Translated from Ukrainian by Daisy Gibbons*

Daisy Gibbons is a prize-winning Ukrainian-to-English literary translator. Her publications include Tamara Duda's Shevchenko Award-winning *Daughter* (Mosaic Press) and a forthcoming book on President Zelensky with Pegasus Books. Her work has appeared in *Harpers*, *Vanity Fair*, and *Los Angeles Review of Books*.

# OKSANA
# LUTSYSHYNA

OKSANA LUTSYSHYNA

Oksana Lutsyshyna is a Ukrainian writer, translator, and poet (b.1974, Uzhhorod). She is the author of three novels, a collection of short stories, and five books of poetry, the latest of them published in English translation in 2019 (*Persephone Blues*, Arrowsmith). For her latest novel, *Ivan and Phoebe*, which almost documentally describes the events of The Revolution on Granite, she was awarded two of the most prestigious literary awards in Ukraine: the Lviv City of Literature UNESCO Prize (2020) and the Taras Shevchenko National Award in fiction (2021). She holds a PhD in Comparative Literature and is currently a lecturer in Ukrainian Studies at the University of Texas at Austin, where she teaches the Ukrainian language and Eastern European literature in translation.

Since 2000, Lutsyshyna has been working in the field of feminist-centric literature. According to Oksana Lutsyshyna, in her novellas she tries to recreate the female world as it is, regardless of any prescriptions and rules, without thematic and stylistic restrictions. Her poetry is often characterful, combining an elegant form and intellectual tension with emotionality and passion. In her writing, Lutsyshyna

272

combines Western discourse and Ukrainian poetic tradition. Oksana Lutsyshina also translates poetry and essays by Ukrainian authors into English, as well as American poets' work into Ukrainian.

Having lived for a significant length of time in the United States, Lutsyshyna often finds herself called upon to represent her homeland and explain Ukraine abroad.

\*\*\*

and a knight steps out into the ring – that is
there is no ring at all,
and speaks with him – with whom?
a muteness with no name:
you must make the right choice knight
if you go right – you'll lose your cat
if you go left – you'll lose your cat
whichever way you chose to go,
you'll lose your cat

because you are a knight only in your dreams
in visions while you sleep
and really all that you possess, has already
been written on the wall
and the wall is like a cliff
like solitude itself
*mene tekel feres*

because you're really not a knight but a woman
not a woman of ages past
and if you find yourself in an arena or ring
its only because the Good Lord
sends you these visions, dreams
against the army of separation
sends it straight into your head
straight into your facebook

and when you take your hands off the steering wheel

and when you sleeplessly slumber
at the edge of an invisible cliff as if
exhausted from sightseeing
He makes you remember – here I am
your muteness is at its height
and wherever you go
or run from danger
you will still lose your cat

but you'll never lose Me
across all the ages
and so rise, knight, and
here I am – a sign
rise,
God speaks

*2020*

\*\*\*

nothing happens nothing happens
everything is suspended like in Bruno Schultz's July night
maybe because mercury is in retrograde
but why the hell does all life
seem like it's all in a mercury retrograde
aren't there planets
other than this mercury…

no one comes nothing comes
not even the damn mail comes
only some coupons for pizza

in fact this is an improvement
at least they're not for vinegar from a Soviet era shop

near the churches they once put out stones
large boulders
for those who needed to cry but didn't know where
or how
the boulders called them with their boulder voices

it said – I will be the heart of your summer

the heart of a July night

*2020*

***

here is how a city feels under siege
in the heart of its most central square
it is injured as if it's been burned
as if for days someone has been splashing and splashing it
        with scalding water or tar
because the enemy forces are far away but the scalding
        water is close
and they can't leave off doing this until tomorrow

there its dogs howl and their horses go mad in their stalls
there they feel the full moon and can't break through to it
there they howl in chorus, what did St. Augustine say
        about breath?

there its walls move like waves
like the ocean waves from a submerged volcano
and the waves, like walls, move forward and backward
the waves, like enemies, bringing anger and hope

how long will this city survive, the moon says
well, what if forever? and if it doesn't get better,
        if it lasts and lasts – the burning, the waves
and whatever else
can happen to a city under siege? will you make it?
and you exhale and say, firmly looking into its one eye:
I will

*2020*

*Translated from Ukrainian by Olena Jennings and the author*

Olena Jennings is the author of the poetry collections *The Age of Secrets* (Lost Horse Press) and *Songs from an Apartment*. Her novel *Temporary Shelter* was released in 2021 from Cervena Barva Press. Her translation of Vasyl Makhno's poetry collection, *Paper Bridge*, was published by Plamen Press and her translation with Oksana Lutsyshyna of Kateryna Kalytko's collection *Nobody Knows Us Here and We Don't Know Anyone* is forthcoming from Lost Horse Press. She is the founder and curator of the Poets of Queens reading series and press.

# VASYL
# MAKHNO

VASYL MAKHNO

A Ukrainian poet, prose writer, essayist, and translator (b.1964, Chortkiv), Makhno is the author of fourteen collections of poetry, the most recent of which is *One Sail House* (2021). Two poetry collections, *Thread and Other New York Poems* (2009) and *Winter Letters* (2011), have appeared in English, and a third, *Paper Bridge* (2022), was published by Plamen Press in English translation by Olena Jennings. Makhno is the recipient of Kovaliv Fund Prize (2008, USA), Serbia's International Povele Morave Prize in Poetry (2013), the BBC Book of the Year Award (Ukraine, 2015), and the 2020 "Encounter: The Ukrainian-Jewish Literary Prize™" for his first novel *Vichnyi Kalendar* (*The Eternal Calendar*).

Makhno currently lives with his family in New York City, where he moved in 2000. This move coincided with a fundamental change in his writing—from a symbolic modernist-style of poetry to a more direct representation of Western tradition style. Becoming a poetic chronicler of New York City and its specific urban space, he remains intimately connected to Ukraine, which is reflected in his poetry, essays, and a novel.

Makhno's texts are intellectually dense, aphoristic, and saturated with metaphors and cultural allusions. His works have been translated into more than twenty languages, and his books have been published in Europe and the United States.

## LITERATURE AND WAR

In the early Middle Ages, in addition to the obvious soldiers, poets and chroniclers—people of letters—took part in military campaigns in order to first and foremost record the particulars of the military operations, to praise the wise and fearless monarch, and to sing the warriors' victories. If it is indeed authentic, our *Tale of Ihor's Campaign*[37] is about precisely this. So literature served war and war became a source for compilations of poetic and historic chronicles, thorough or not. Over time, everything got more complicated—both war and literature. At the start of the twentieth century, telegraph agencies transmitted their correspondents' reports on various acts of war all around the world. With the development of communications technology, literature fell behind. It required a few years to fully digest what had happened. Of course, poetry reacted faster, but prose, this literary heavyweight, had to first stretch its muscles to make it to the end. The literature of World War I is a perfect example. At first it was written by the people participating in it—the lost generation, who

---

37 An epic poem considered anonymous, written in the Old East Slavic language, which describes an unsuccessful campaign of Igor Svyatoslavich (1185) against the Polovtsians of the Don River region.

was then eighteen to twenty years old. Later it became the object of observation by those who hadn't participated, and much later by the next generations of writers. The contributions of the Americans Erich Maria Remarque, Osyp Turiansky, Marko Cheremshyna, Jaroslav Hašek, Guillaume Apollinaire, and Nikolai Gumilev got the most attention. As well as those of poet Georg Trakl, killed in war, and the physically unharmed philosopher Ludwig Wittgenstein, who equally hated war and served in the military not out of desire, but out of obligation. An obligation that all states proclaim sacred, and so then threaten deserters and resisters with imprisonment or death.

The semantics of war are always the same: it has its economic, psychological, and demographic elements. There must be various contradictions of a social nature; territorial infringement; the desire to capture, control, and enrich under the guise of propagandistic slogans specially prepared for these cases. In general, after the declaration of war and the first military operations in Europe, WWI naturally divided the intellectuals of the time. Writers and philosophers were in opposite camps: those who for patriotic reasons exalted the strength of national forces and those who saw inhumane absurdity in yet more worldwide bloodshed. Of course, this scattered chorus was joined by the members of the socialist and communist parties who ostensibly cared about the interests of the world proletariat—their benefit and positions are a topic for another conversation. Obviously the openly pacifist views of the Russian writing couple Merezhkovsky and Gippius or the German Herman Hesse, who published an article entitled "O Friends, Not These Sounds!", were incomprehensible to Ernest Hemingway, Remarque, or Nikolai Gumilov and other young volunteers, who saw the war as a way to achieve glory and that adrenaline of utmost importance to the young body. Understanding and disappointment would come later when *A Farewell to Arms* and *All Quiet on the Western Front* were written. These novels feature the everyday brutality of the military alongside the crushing of illusions.

The experience of war does not pass an entire generation or even an individual without leaving a trace. The events of World War II also had to wait dozens of years before Henrich Böll, Vasil Bykaŭ, Günter Grass, and Viktor Astafyev attempted to make sense out of their participation in the largest war in the history of civilization. It is also worth mentioning that all war literature can be divided into the experience of the victors and the trauma of the vanquished. Many works from other literary regions, in particular Japanese and Chinese writers, are dedicated to the Second Sino–Japanese War. For example, the writer Ashihei Hino glorifies Japanese militarism, which his fellow countryman Jun Ishikawa condemns. Fighters from both sides of a conflict experience trauma, for every army has its dead and wounded, its looters and rapists, and ultimately, its heroes and traitors.

It is worth reflecting on why Ukrainian literature has been denied the chance to seriously reflect on the events of World War II. Or has it refused on its own? Was there in fact a civil war in 1917? Both Mykola Khvylovy and Yuri Yanovsky, among others, showed clashes within Ukrainian society, reaching stylistic and psychological depths in their portrayals. But how telling is the fact that when Yanovsky decided to truly illustrate the consequences of the Second World War for Ukraine with his novel *Living Water*, it was bowdlerized into the unrecognizable *Peace*? Or Dovzhenko and his extremely frank journal entries? It is clear that before World War I, the territory of contemporary Ukraine was split among empires for whose tsar and kaiser Ukrainians had to die on the front. In contrast, during World War I the sentiments of the people varied much more than it might seem at first glance. After the Holodomor, forced collectivization, the purges, and mass arrests in Stalin's Soviet Union, the number of those in the territory of Soviet Ukraine who despised the Bolsheviks grew. Many Galicians served in the Polish army in interwar Poland, but starting in 1939, the USSR began conscripting Galician youths to the Red Army. I can understand, then, the hopes Ukrainian nationalists placed on the idea floating around at the time of a new war that would put an end to the battles with Poland *and* the Soviets. It was impossible to depict this interweaving of ideologies, moods, and events under the harsh censorship of Soviet Ukrainian literature, so it turned out one-sided, false, and sterile.

Galician literature was crushed in 1939. In the 60s there were attempts to show the complexity of the situation, mostly in works about Galicia[38] and Volhynia.[39]

---

38 A historical region of northwestern Ukraine that borders Polissia in the north, and Podillia and Galicia in the south. The Uzh and Western Buh rivers are considered the eastern and western borders. According to Encyclopedia of Ukraine, its area is approximately 70,000 sq km.
39 A historical and geographical region of southwestern Ukraine and southeastern Poland. According to Encyclopedia of Ukraine, it has an area of 55,700 sq km. The name comes from the medieval city of Halych.

That is, in writing about these places, it was impossible to ignore these intricacies, but the Soviet censors ripped apart everything that seemed suspicious. To the very end Günter Grass hid his membership in the Waffen-SS,[40] though Henrich Böll, who was a soldier in the Wehrmacht, wrote openly about his part in the war. He was one of the first to stand up for the kind of reimagining of German literature and its language that Group 47[41] pursued. Because the war, roughly speaking, didn't end with the signing of an instrument of surrender. It didn't end for anyone—not for Böll, nor Grass, not for Paul Celan and his Jewish sorrow, labor camps in Transnistria, and ashes of memory. The war didn't end for Vasiliy Grosman or Vasil Bykaŭ, who fought in that fixed fight for every scene and every sentence.

My generation had another war, the war in Afghanistan, the largest of all the local conflicts in which the Soviet Union ever intervened. And that list is quite long—Korea, Vietnam, events in Angola, and other African and Asian countries—always with deceitful assurances about preserving and fighting for peace. In 1979, continuing the policy of supporting illusory socialist revolutions, the USSR took a limited (as they then wrote in the papers) contingent of troops into this Muslim country to help the brotherly Afghan people preserve the gains of the Saur Revolution. Soon rumors spread through our cities and towns that the first casualties had returned from Afghanistan. The Soviet army, with all its problems—

---

40 Combat branch of the Nazi Party's Schutzstaffel (SS) organization.
41 German literary group initiated by Hans Werner Richter between 1947–1967. It became a platform for the renewal of German literature after World War II.

drunkenness, hazing, crime, tyranny of command—found itself in a real war for the first time since 1945. What does Ukrainian literature have to say about it? Works started coming out later during *perestroika*. Does anyone remember them? I'm not sure. There was no deficit of non-fiction or memoirs written by veterans of the war, which satisfied the need for national memory of the war. But artistic memory with its aesthetic dimension, which has a different nature and task in comparison to reporting, again failed to materialize.

But then, unexpectedly, on the eve of the year 2014 as a result of letting the modern Ukrainian army reach rock bottom, as a result of betrayal and corruption and thanks to direct Russian support and invasion, the Donbas and Luhansk regions were bloodied and Crimea annexed. So here on the edge of Europe, just like during the collapse of Yugoslavia, of course with a slightly different course of events, Ukraine started carrying out military actions on its own territory against separatists. Poetry immediately reacted to the events on the Maidan, and then to the battles in Sloviansk, Ilovaisk, and other towns. There were so many poems—written by children who sent greeting cards to soldiers on the front and by poets who felt compelled to express their civic position. Prose caught up later, coming not only from writers, but also from veterans, journalists, and simply people who cared and suddenly felt the irresistible urge to write.

With a few exceptions, the literature on this topic isn't outstanding. The cinema is better, perhaps because the brutality of the time requires more visualization. Perhaps this is a new rule for our time, which thanks to all its gadgets has managed to harm the aesthetics of the word to a certain degree. Perhaps the demand of Roman citizens—bread and circuses—is actually more concerned with the circuses, and new technology brings us closer to events while leaving us on the other side of the screen, that is, in safety. Behind the descriptions of war, are only descriptions; underneath the topsoil of words are only the roots of grass. As long as humanity exists, there will be wars, as well as attempts to preserve all this dirt in writing. We, therefore, cannot avoid the question, "What will our literature and language look like after the war?"

*January, 2021*

*Translated from Ukrainian by Ali Kinsella*

A former Peace Corps volunteer, Ali Kinsella has been translating from Ukrainian since 2012, and her work has appeared in *Solstice*, *Kenyon Review*, *Apofenie*, and *Guernica*. *Eccentric Days of Hope and Sorrow: Selected Poems by Natalka Bilotserkivets*, a collection she co-translated with Dzvinia Orlowsky (Lost Horse Press, 2021) is a finalist for the 2022 Griffin Poetry Prize.

# ACKNOWLEDGMENTS

This book could not have possibly happened without the help and support of extraordinary people—our advisors, colleagues, and friends. We are deeply grateful to Bridget Matzie, the partner at Aevitas Creative literary agency, who helped launch this effort and guided us through the complex publishing process. Special thanks to the ambassador of *Craft Magazine* and Vice President of People and Culture at Atlantic Group, Christi Anne Hofland, for her help with contacting literary translators. We are indebted to Maria Genkin, Razom for Ukraine board member, for bringing more attention to this book among the international audience.

We especially thank our Ukrainian friends and colleagues for helping us to establish new contacts with contributors and with text selection—Svitlana Oleshko, a screenwriter, director, author of documentaries, and founder of one of the most famous independent Ukrainian experimental theaters, Kharkiv theater "Arabesques," and Bohdana Neborak, a journalist, manager of cultural projects, and editor at "The Ukrainians" media.

This collection could not be fully representative without beautiful portraits of the contributors. We are incredibly grateful to Valentyn Kuzan, a documentary and portrait photographer with whom we have been working since 2020 and who is the author of almost all the portraits in this book. Also, we thank Kateryna Lashchykova for S. Aseyev's photo, Nastya Telikova for O. Herasymyuk's photo, Sofiya Soliar (The Ukrainians) for I. Kalynets's photo, and authors (I. Andrusiak, O. Stiazhkina, L. Deresh, V. Makhno, K. Moskalets, V. Rafeyenko, O. Chupa) for providing photos from their personal collections.

We express our gratitude to the publishing houses that granted us the rights to translate and print some works: Suhrkamp Verlag for Serhiy Zhadan's poems (originally published in Ukrainian by Meridian Czernowitz); The Old Lion Publishing House for Andriy Bondar's essay "Eternal Memory" from the collection *I tym, shcho v hrobakh* (*And for Those in the Graves*, 2016), Pavlo Korobchuk's poem "Letter from a Sailor to his Daughter" from the collection *Khvoia* (*Needles*, 2017), and Yuliya Musakovska's poems from the collection *Men, Women and Children* (2015); A-ba-ba-ha-la-ma-ga Publishing House for Ivan Malkovych's poems, and Luta Sprava Publishing for an excerpt from Olaf Clemensen's *Summer-ATO* (2015).

There would literally not be a book without incredible literary translation. We are infinitely grateful to our translators for their instant consent to join the project and their hard work. We thank our editor at 8th & Atlas Publishing, Christina De Paris, for her faith in this project, as well as her patience and perseverance in editing this book.

Finally, we are deeply grateful to our families and friends. Kateryna thanks David Holmes for reading and editing earlier drafts of the manuscript, enduring inspiration, and support.

# ABOUT THE EDITORS

Kateryna Kazimirova is an editor and media manager. She holds Master's degrees in Philology (Ukrainian Language and Literature) and History of Art and a Postgraduate degree in Literary Theory from Vasyl' Stus Donetsk National University. In 2020, she founded the Ukrainian art and literature journal *Craft Magazine* (craftmagazine. net), which publishes in-depth interviews with the most talented and creative Ukrainians to showcase to the world the leading voices of modern, free Ukraine. At the time of its founding, *Craft Magazine* was the only publication of this format that featured an English version of all texts.

Daryna Anastasieva is a journalist, co-founding editor of *Craft Magazine*, and head of the Radio PR Department in *Suspilne Ukraine* (Public Broadcast Company of Ukraine). She received a Master's degree in History of Ukrainian Literature at Vasyl' Stus Donetsk National University. Anastasieva is a communications specialist, manager of cultural projects, and producer of creative studios and events.

Christina De Paris is a publisher, philanthropist, and multimedia creator. She obtained a B.A. in Journalism and an M.S. in Global Studies and has had her translations, graphic designs, and writing published by various groups, including the United Nations and Sweden's foreign affairs magazine, *Utrikesmagasinet*. Christina founded 8th & Atlas Publishing in 2020 with her two brothers, Michael and Brent, and published a short stories collection, *Around the Cul-de-sac*, in 2021.

# Voices of Freedom

## CONTEMPORARY WRITING
## FROM UKRAINE

www.8thandatlaspublishing.com

www.ingramcontent.com/pod-product-compliance
Lightning Source LLC
Chambersburg PA
CBHW051126190726
48290CB00006B/1711